Mary Cecilia Caddell

Tales of the Festivals

Mary Cecilia Caddell

Tales of the Festivals

ISBN/EAN: 9783743332874

Manufactured in Europe, USA, Canada, Australia, Japa

Cover: Foto ©Andreas Hilbeck / pixelio.de

Manufactured and distributed by brebook publishing software
(www.brebook.com)

Mary Cecilia Caddell

Tales of the Festivals

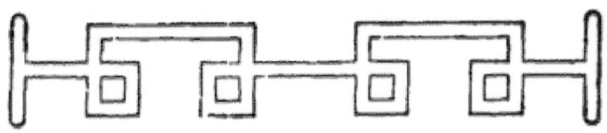

Ash-Wednesday.[*]

All hail, Jesus! Mary, all hail!

"HOW dull it will be to-morrow!" said little Nina one evening, as she and Madeleine sat at supper with Marie, while Father Pierre and the elders of the party chatted round the fire.

"And why should it be so dull to-morrow?" asked Marie, in great surprise.

"Oh, because I always think every one looks so cold and hungry on Ash-Wednesday," answered Nina. "And then the great black patch on their foreheads makes them look so dismal."

"Black patch on their foreheads!" cried Marie; "what do you mean, Nina? Shall we have black patches on our foreheads to-morrow?"

* Continued from "the Purification."

"Yes, to be sure," persisted Nina; "we go up to the altar, and the priest makes the sign of the cross on our foreheads with ashes; and it looks for all the world just like a great black patch over one's nose. Where have you lived all your life, Marie, not to know that?"

Marie coloured a little, but Madeleine came to her assistance.

"And pray how should she know any thing about it, when she never was able to go to Church in all her life on Ash-Wednesday? for Minette has often told me so?"

"You will tell me all about it, without laughing at me, dear Madeleine," said Marie. "Why will Father Pierre put ashes on our foreheads to-morrow?"

Madeleine hesitated a moment, and then she said, "In the first place, Marie, I believ it is to put us in mind that we all must die, because the priest always says while he signs the cross on our forehead, 'Remember. man, thou art but dust, and unto dust thou shalt return.'"

"Well," said Marie.

"Well," said her friend, laughing at her

eagerness. "In the second place, I .hink it is to warn us, that as we are sinners, we ought to do penance for our sins; and we are naturally more willing to do this, when we reflect that every day may be the last of our lives, and that we shall have to suffer in the next world for the sins which we have not atoned for by our mortifications in this one."

"But why should ashes put us in mind of doing penance?" said Nina; "I do not see what they have to do with one's sins, or to one's doing penance for them either."

"Father Pierre told me yesterday," answered Madeleine, "that in the olden times ashes were always used as a sign of sorrow or of repentance. And he says it is mentioned in the Bible, that holy Job put ashes on his head as a mark of suffering, when God struck him with ulcers from head to foot. And also that when the prophet Jonas preached to the inhabitants of the city of Nineveh, they wore sackcloth, and covered themselves with ashes, in token of their sorrow for their sins."

"Certainly," said Marie, "it seems very right that if we commit sin, we should do

pei ance for it, because even quite little children are punished by their mothers whenever
they do any thing naughty."

"And we are all of us, both old and young,
the little children of our Heavenly Father,"
said Father Pierre, who had been silently listening to the children as they sat chatting together. "Let us be thankful to this good and
tender Parent, who, in amends for our many
ingratitudes towards Him, asks nothing more
dismal of us than fasting some few days in
the year, and receiving ashes on our foreheads
on a cold spring morning." He smiled, and
laid his hand upon Nina's head, as he finished
his speech. She grew scarlet in a moment,
but then, with a great effort of courage, she
said, "Well but, Father Pierre, it must be very
disagreeable to go without one's breakfast in
the morning,—and people always look as if
they thought so too"—she added, growing
bolder as she detected another smile on the
good father's face. "Very likely they do,"
he answered, now laughing outright; "for a
good breakfast is a very good thing, and not
at all to be despised · but let me tell you some-

thing, my little Nina, which I think would reconcile even you to the disagreeable necessity of going without your breakfast during the dismal days of Lent."

"Oh, do tell it to us, sir," said Madeleine; "for I confess I often think I shall not like fasting much better than Nina does, whenever I am old enough to be obliged to keep Lent."

Father Pierre answered very gravely; "The sweet Jesus fasted for us forty days and forty nights in the desert. He neither eat nor drank during all that time, lying on the bare ground, and having, as St. Luke tells us, brute beasts for His sole companions. When we fast, we try to imitate Jesus, and to become like to Him. And we must never forget that the more we resemble Him, the dearer we become to our Heavenly Father, who has declared by the Holy Ghost Himself, 'This is My beloved Son, in whom I am well pleased.'"

"Ah, if fasting makes us dear to Jesus and our Heavenly Father, I should be very glad to begin to-morrow," whispered Marie.

"After Jesus had fasted forty days in the desert," continued Father Pierre, "Scripture

tells us He was tempted by the ~evil; and
this He permitted in order to show us how
needful it is for us to mortify our bodies, if we
wish firmly to resist our natural inclination tc
evil."

"And was our Blessed Saviour the first
person who ever fasted, Father Pierre?"

"Certainly not, my dear child. Fasting
was very common among the Jews, either on
occasions of private sorrow or of public repentance. Besides these, which were only volun-
tary, the law of Moses ordained a general fast
on one particular day of the year, which was
for this reason called the day of atonement."

"But were little children obliged to fast
under the old law, Father Pierre?" asked
Madeleine, with a sly glance at her sister.

"Not absolutely to fast," he answered, almost laughing at little Nina's look of conster
nation; "but when ever a Jewish mother consecrated one of her children to God (as was
sometimes the case), she was obliged to make
it abstain from wine and certain kinds of meat.
Such a child was called a Nazarite, that is,
one set aside in a particular manner to God."

"St. John the Baptist must have fasted when he was quite a child," continued Made leine; "for dear old Madame Margaret once told me he went into the desert when he was only five years old, and that he lived there on locusts and wild honey."

"Well," cried Nina, "the wild honey was not so bad;—but the locusts! they must have been very nasty indeed, Madeleine."

"Console yourself, my dear child," said the good father, drawing the little girl gently towards him; "we shall not ask you to give up your breakfast, or even to feed upon honey and locusts. But there is one kind of mortification which even little children may and ought to practise at all times of the year, and more especially during the holy time of Lent."

"Oh, do tell us, Father Pierre," cried Marie and Madeleine in the same instant.

Father Pierre tried to look very grave, but there was a smile lurking in the corner of his mouth, as he answered, "Why, I think it would be very bad indeed for my poor little Nina to go without her breakfast these cold and hungry-looking mornings; but I do not fancy it would do her any harm, indeed I almost imagine it would be very good for her chest and lungs, if she would try and refrain from the passion of tears in which she sometimes chooses to indulge."

"Oh! Father Pierre," cried Nina, almost sobbing as she spoke, "did you really see me crying yesterday morning?"

"Yes, my child," said the Father, kindly but gravely, "I did; and when I again passed by the door of your cottage, three-quarters of an hour afterwards, you were still in tears; but so busy rubbing your eyes and tearing your hair, that you did not even see me."

"It was because I was not allowed to go with Madeleine to see Marie," poor Nina answered in a tone of excuse.

"Well, Nina," answered Father Pierre, "should such a misfortune occur again during the time of Holy Lent, try and take it as a little penance sent you, instead of the fast imposed upon your elders. Remember, that if your Heavenly Father does not require little children to fast, He at least expects them to be always cheerfully obedient to the will of their superiors."

"I have read in some good book," said Minette, "that every one should sanctify the Lent by taking some particular fault, and trying to conquer it."

"Your good book was quite in the right," answered Father Pierre. "The fast from sin is the great object of our Lenten mortifications, and the fast from food is chiefly to be considered as a means for obtaining this great end."

"That is, I suppose," said old Martha, "because Almighty God rewards our penance by granting us a greater grace to resist temptation."

"Besides this additional grace, which is certainly given," observed the Father, "the soul also acquires a greater command over the body; for if she can compel it to refrain from food, which is its most natural inclination, she can surely curb it in its more evil propensities. It is therefore an excellent plan to take some particular fault, and to try and subdue it during this holy season, when additional graces are given us for the purpose. Therefore, I am quite sure that my little Nina will now really begin to conquer her temper; Madeleine will be more orderly in the care of the household; and Marie will never be so late for Mass as she was yesterday morning."

' That was my fault, Father Pierre," said Madeleine eagerly; "she called for me, and I asked her to wait until I had finished the kitchen.   Because I was too late that morning," she added, with a blush.

"Well," said Father Pierre, smiling, "next time, I advise her not to wait for you, because we are not to do what is wrong, even to please our friends; and we must all, both young and old, remember that we are bound to try, at least, and lead more pure and holy lives in Lent; those who keep the fast, in order to sanctify it; and those who are not able to do so, in order to make up for it."

" Besides trying to lead better lives," said Minette, "I suppose people who are not able to fast, ought to do some other good work instead, during Lent."

"They certainly should say some additional prayers," answered the Father; "and if they are rich enough, they ought to be very liberal to the poor during this holy season. I am also much inclined to advise those who do not fast, to refrain from the more dainty and agreeable kinds of food, both because they share by this means in the mortifications of those who fast, and because I believe a simple diet is, generally speaking, the most conducive to health and strength."

"I believe the primitive Christians observed Lent much more strictly than we do. Did they not, Father Pierre?" asked Minette.

"They never even dreamed of taking food before evening, Minette; and those who did so at an earlier hour, were not considered, and did not consider themselves, as fasting."

"But, Father Pierre, who made us keep Lent first?" asked Nina; "was it our Blessed Saviour?"

"I think I might almost say it was; for when the disciples of John came to Him, saying, 'Why do we and the Pharisees fast often, and your disciples do not fast?' He answered that His disciples should fast when the Bridegroom was taken from them."

"That is, when He went up into Heaven, I suppose," said Minette.

"Just so, Minette. The Apostles without doubt fasted often in obedience to this command of their Divine Master, and we find the observance of Lent clearly mentioned by all ecclesiastical writers, even by those of the first century, when the immediate disciples of the apostles were still alive."

"But were not people made to do public penance in those days, Father Pierre?"

"Those who were conscious of any great sin made their confessions before Lent began, and on Ash-Wednesday they repaired to the church-door bare-footed and dressed in mean and torn garments, such as were then always used for mourning. As soon as they were admitted into the church, they prostrated themselves on the ground, and, with many tears and expressions of sorrow, begged to be received to penance and absolution. The Bishop then gave them ashes to strew on their heads, and sackcloth to cover their bodies, and after saying the penitential psalms over them, he and the clergy laid their hands upon them, in order to confirm this dedication of themselves to penance. He also made them a moving exhortation, telling them that as Adam was expelled from Paradise in punishment of his sin, so they were now going to be driven for a time from the church; but at the same time he always encouraged them most affectionately to persevere in doing penance, by the hopes he held out of the Divine forgiveness, which in this manner they would certainly succeed in obtaining. Then he pushed them from him, and bade the inferior ministers drive them out of the church. The clergy followed them to the door, repeat ing this responsory to them, 'In the sweat of thy face thou shalt eat thy bread; for dust thou art, and unto dust thou shalt return.' These penances did not finish with the Lent in which they were begun, and they often lasted for many years."

"And were they never allowed to enter the church all that time?" cried Marie; "oh, Father Pierre, how very dreadful!"

"In the first year of their penance they were called Weepers," answered Father Pierre, "and during the hours of prayer they stood in the

porch, clothed in sackcloth, and having ashes
on their heads, imploring the prayers of the
faithful who entered the church. After they
had passed some time fervently in this class,
they were received by the Bishop into the
second order of penitents, called Hearers, because they were allowed to enter the church
in order to attend to the sermon, but were
obliged to depart before any of the prayers
were begun. From this rank they advanced
into that of Prostrators, who remained prostrate on the floor of the church while certain
prayers were said for them: and they afterwards passed into the fourth class of penitents,
called Consistents, who joined in prayer with
the rest of the Christians, but were not allowed
to make their offering, or to receive the Holy
Communion. After they had fully accomplished this penance of many years, they were once
more brought to the church on Maunday-
Thursday, and publicly absolved by the Bishop,
who made them hold up their hands as a token
of their resolution to lead new lives for the fu
ture."

"But then every one must have known by

this public penance, if one had been guilty of serious sin, and that was not very pleasant, I think," said Minette.

"The Christians of those days, Minette, were so much in love with the cross of Jesus Christ that they often undertook these acts of public humiliation, without having been guilty of the crimes for which they were ordained. It was therefore impossible to distinguish betwixt those who did penance by command of the Bishop, and those who performed it as a private devotion."

"I have heard this given as a reason why the Church no longer enforces public penance," said Dame Martha, "Is this really the case, Father Pierre?"

"I think it a very sufficient one," he answered. "Sin is always equally hateful in the sight of God; therefore, the amount of punishment incurred by its commission must ever remain the same; but, as few would of their own accord do penance in this cold unfervent age, its performance would be attended with total loss of character in those upon whom it was enforced; an evil to which our tender mother, the Church, could never expose the most guilty of her children."

"I remember," said Madeleine, "Madame Margaret once told me such a beautiful story about a young lady who did public penance at Rome, with her hair all dishevelled, and her face and hands dirty, and the Bishop and priests and people all weeping around her.

"Her name was Fabiola," said Father Pierre; "and for a fault committed entirely through ignorance, she submitted, in the sight of all Rome, to the severe discipline of canonical penance. The emperor Theodosius has also left us an heroic example of public repentance. He was naturally of a very hasty disposition; and once, in a fit of passion, he punished a revolt of his subjects by a frightful massacre of the innocent as well as of the guilty. St. Ambrose was at that time Bishop of Milan, and, filled with horror at this act of barbarity he left the town in order to avoid seeing the Emperor too soon, and sent him a letter declaring that, until he did penance for his sin, he would neither receive his offering, nor celebrate Mass in his presence. Soon after, he re-

turned to Milan, and the Emperor went as usual
to church; but St. Ambrose met him at the
porch, and forbade him to enter. The prince
said, by way of excuse, that David also had
sinned, and the holy Bishop told him in reply,
that, as he had followed the king of Israel in
sinning, he ought also to follow him in his repentance. Theodosius submitted, and retiring to
his palace, clad himself in mourning weeds, and
passed eight months without once going into
the church. At the end of that time, one of his
courtiers, called Ruffinus, persuaded him to allow him to go and intercede with St. Ambrose
for his forgiveness, and Theodosius, flattering
himself with hopes of success, followed him soon
after. However, when St. Ambrose saw Ruffinus, he spoke to him most severely, and told
him that if Theodosius dared to approach the
church, he would meet him in the porch, and
forbid him to enter; and upon this Ruffinus
instantly sent a messenger to the Emperor, to
tell him what had passed. The good prince
was already in the high-street when he received
the information, but, instead of turning back,
he only said 'I will go and receive the affront

and rebuke I deserve.' He then proceeded to the church, but, without going into it, he besought the Bishop to give him absolution. St. Ambrose asked him what penance he had done, and the Emperor said he was willing to submit to any he might impose. The Bishop then ordered him to place himself among the public penitents. Theodosius instantly complied, and, prostrating himself upon the pavement, remained for a long time weeping and praying, and lamenting his sin in the sight of the people, who were so touched by his humility, that they wept and prayed with him. St. Ambrose tells us, that after he received absolution, he never passed a day of his life without bewailing afresh this crime, into which he had been chiefly led through the instigation of others; and, in obedience to the Bishop's orders, he also made a law commanding a respite of thirty days before the execution of any sentence regarding life or loss of property, so that passion or surprise could never again take the place of justice."

"That was a real blessing to his subjects," Dame Martha observed; "for in thirty days he would have plenty of time to consider whether the sentence he had pronounced was just, and to change it if he found it was not."

" Yes," said Father Pierre; " we have the whole history of the use of penance in this one anecdote of the life of Theodosius. In the first place, it brings us to the resolution to sin no more. In the next, it reconciles us to our Heavenly Father, who, as an expiation for our faults, accepts the trifling sufferings we inflict on our own bodies, united with, and made meritorious by, the passion and death of Jesus Christ. And let us never forget that, without this union, the best of our actions would be entirely worthless in His sight. In the third place, it compels us to repair any injuries we may have done to our neighbours, and teaches us to behave towards them with greater charity for the future."

Marie thought the country looked particularly gloomy the next morning, as she walked with her mother to church, and she could not forbear saying, " Nina was right after all, Mamma; Ash-Wednesday certainly is the most dismal day of the year."

" Well, perhaps it is," said Minette; " but I

daresay the desert was not very pleasant either
and yet Jesus was alone in it for forty days."

"And St. John from the time he was five
years old. Oh! Mamma how could a child of
five years old like to live alone in a desert?"

"No common child could have done so,
Marie; but St. John was a great saint from
the hour of his birth, and therefore, even at
five years old, he loved Jesus so well, that he
liked better to do His Divine will by going
into the desert, than to follow his own by remaining with his parents."

Marie made no answer, but she thought a
great deal during the remainder of her walk,
and she resolved to go without her breakfast
that day for the love of the sweet Jesus, and
in imitation of St. John. She knew she was
not very strong, and therefore she thought it
most likely her mother might not approve of
her intention, and she resolved, if possible, to
conceal it from her. Mary was a very good
little child, but she had yet to learn that obedience is better than sacrifice.

There was no breakfast at the cottage that
morning, so Minette arranged Marie's bread

and milk on a little table near the window, and
then left the room.   Marie sat for a long time
pondering as to how she should conceal the fact
of her having taken no breakfast.   The bread
she could easily cover up in her work-basket,
but she was puzzled what to do with the milk.
Just then a beggar came and stood at the little
garden-gate, and a bright smile crossed Marie's
lips.   " It will be an act of charity and of penance too," thought she ; and putting the bread
into her apron, and spilling half the milk, in her
eagerness to escape, she glided out of the house-
door, and presented them to the poor man.

He received them with a look of surprise ;
but with a smile that went quite to her heart,
as he answered—" I thank you, dear little
child, but I never drink milk on Ash-Wednesday ; nor do I break my fast until sunset."

" But you *must* take them from me," Marie
answered eagerly.   " Put the bread into your
wallet, and there—you have a leathern bottle
at your girdle, pour the milk into that."   She
did all this herself while she was speaking, and
then, still scarlet with excitement, ran off to
join Madeleine, whom she saw a few paces

down the street, coming to take her to school.

Marie could not settle to her lessons that morning; her stomach was sick, and her head so giddy she could not see the letters in her book; and at last she covered her face with her hands, and cried herself to sleep. It is not, therefore, surprising, that when her class was called to say their lessons to Sister Mary Aloysia, she did not know a word of them. It was a very unusual occurrence with her, and she was sentenced to kneel for penance in the middle of the room. Poor Marie! She felt the disgrace most acutely, but she did not like to plead sickness as an excuse for her idleness; so she knelt down without remonstrance; but she had not been a minute on her knees, before she fainted. When she opened her eyes again, she found herself sitting at an open window, Mary Aloysia and Madeleine were kneeling beside her; the nun gave her a glass of water with a little wine in it, and then she felt quite revived again. "I know why you fainted, Marie," cried Madeleine; "you have had no breakfast this morning; I saw you giving yours to a poor man at the door."

"No breakfast!" said the nun; "my dear child, why did you not say so before? You must have some directly." She left the room as she spoke; but soon returned with a cup of coffee and some bread and butter, which she placed before Marie. The little girl still hesitated; she did not like to give up her fast. "But, dear Sister Mary Aloysia," she ventured at last to say, "it was not only for charity that I gave my breakfast to the poor man; it was also because I wanted to fast."

"My dear child," said the smiling nun, "you are much too young to think of fasting."

"But St. John fasted when he was much younger than I am."

"Because he *was* St. John," said Mary Aloysia, more gravely. "The life which he ed was a direct inspiration from Almighty God; but, do you think that if the sweet Jesus had been with him, and had told him to break his fast, he would have objected to do so?"

"Oh, no, surely not," cried Marie and Madeleine both at the same moment.

"Well, my dear child, religion tells us to look upon the wishes of our superiors as the commands of Jesus Christ Himself. Therefore, when I tell you to take your breakfast directly, I do not think you will disobey me."

Marie did not hesitate another moment, and, to say the truth, she felt all the better for the coffee and bread and butter. As soon as she had finished it, she said, " But, dear Sister Mary Aloysia, why are grown-up people made to fast, and little children are not allowed to do so ?"

" My dear child, the chief merit of the fast of Lent consists in the obedience thus given to the laws of our holy mother, the Church. Now, can you tell me why God forbade our first parents to eat an apple in the garden of paradise ?"

" No, indeed I cannot dear Sister Mary Aloysia," said Marie.

" It was not because the apple was better or worse than any other fruit in the garden," continued the nun. " It was simply because Almighty God desired their obedience on this point, as a proof of the submission of their will to His."

" Then I suppose," said Madeleine, " children obey the Church by not fasting, as much as grown-up people obey by fasting."

"They cannot be said to obey the Church by not fasting, because, in fact, she has given .hem no command either for it or against it. In all these matters children ought to allow them-selves to be guided by their superiors; but I should very much approve of their living on plain food during Lent, if they themselves are willing to give up some little dainties for the sake of the sweet Jesus, who sacrificed Himself so entirely for their sakes while upon earth."

"Then I may do that at least, Sister Mary Aloysia, may I not?" asked Marie anxiously.

"Certainly, my dear child; and if you make obedience your favourite virtue during Lent, if you study to obey instantly and without a murmur the slightest wishes of your superiors, you will be complying, as far as you can, with the *intentions* of the Church, which commands us to fast, chiefl, in order to give us the meri' of obedience. I advise you also to accept ir the spirit of self-mortification any little pen ance that may be imposed upon you during the time of Holy Lent."

"That puts me in mind," said Marie, witl a deep blush, "that I ought to go and knee.

m the middle of the room, because that was
the penance you gave me for not knowing my
lessons, Sister Mary Aloysia."

"But I did not know you were sick, my
dear child, or I should never have desired you
to do so."

"But it was my own fault if I was sick,"
said Marie, with a still deeper blush; "because I knew my mother would not have allowed me to go without my breakfast, and I
half felt all the time that I was disobedient in
attempting to do so."

"And you see now, my dear child, the
danger of following your own will in prefer-
ence to that of the persons whom God has
placed over you. The Church does not consider little children strong enough to fast, yet
you attempted to do so in opposition to the
wishes of your mother, and by this means
rendered yourself incapable of learning your
lessons, which was, however, a positive duty,
since it was commanded by your superiors.
In other words, you preferred a devout practice to a real obligation; but, as your motive
was very good, and you only acted wrong

from want of a little reflection, I shall leave it
to yourself either to finish your penance or
not, just as you please."

"Well, then," said Marie, very humbly, "I
will go to the schoolroom and finish it now,
because I know I deserve it for my disobedi-
ence; and besides, if I must not fast, it will at
least be doing some kind of penance for Ash-
Wednesday, will it not, Sister Mary Aloysia?"

"It will, my child, and the very best kind
of penance too; for when we humble ourselves
before others, we are making some sort of resemblance betwixt ourselves and the sweet
Jesus, who chose for our instruction to be despised as the most abject of men. Remember,
that if He fasted forty days in the desert, He
spent two and thirty years in the constant
practice of humility, and you may judge by
this which of the two virtues He esteems the
most."

Marie waited to hear no more, but instantly
left the room to place herself on her knees
before the wondering gaze of the other children, who had never seen her in disgrace
before.

"I think Marie is a real little angel," whis-pered Madeleine to Sister Mary Aloysia.

"She is a very good child," said the nun; "but she must not attempt great things before she has learned to do little ones well. The saints themselves only became saints by almost imperceptible degrees."

"Yet some of them became good quite sud-denly, Sister Mary Aloysia."

"Some of them, certainly; but I speak of those who were good from their childhood; and if you read their lives carefully, you will see that they almost always began by being very attentive at their prayers and studies, and obedient to their superiors. It was as a re-ward for their practice of these common, easy virtues, that they were inspired to undertake those which were difficult and uncommon."

"I see," said Madeleine, with a sigh; "be-cause they were faithful in little things, God gave them grace to perform those which were greater. I wish I also could be faithful in the litttle things, dear Sister Mary Aloysia."

"You will be faithful if you really wish to be so, my child," said the good nun. "And now, go and tell Marie to come to me; I do not wish her to remain long on her knees after her fainting-fit this morning."

When Marie returned home from school hat evening, she thought she heard a sharp voice in the kitchen; and half-opening the door, she perceived the very poor man to whom she had given her breakfast that morning. He was very tall and thin; and as he stood leaning against the wall, his white hair falling on his shoulders, and his hand grasping a long staff, surmounted by an iron cross, she thought she had never seen any one so like the picture of an old saint before.

"Come in, Marie," cried Minette joyfully; "and ask this good pilgrim to give you his beads to kiss; they have touched the Sepulchre of Jesus Christ."

"But what made you think of going there, sir?" said Marie timidly, as she knelt to kiss the precious chaplet; "it is such a long way off!"

"My child," said the old man sadly, "in my youth I committed a great crime; and when God gave me grace to repent, I felt that

no penance of the old Christian times would
have been too severe for such wickedness as
mine. While in this frame of mind, I resolved
to make a pilgrimage to Jerusalem, and to implore pardon on the very spot where Christ
had suffered and died for my sins. That very
day I began my journey; and if I could not
imitate the wonderful austerities of the saints
of old, I tried at least to cherish something of
that spirit of humility and grief, which made
them appear in the church on Ash-Wednesday, only to be expelled from thence in sackcloth and in ashes."

"And did you really succeed in going so
far as Jerusalem?"

"I have kissed the ground once purpled by
His blood," said the pilgrim, in a voice of deep
emotion; "and there where *He* wept, and
prayed, and died for my salvation, I have
heard the words of absolution pronounced
upon me; and have hoped in that thrice-
blessed moment that 'there was joy in heaven
among the angels of God over one sinner
doing penance upon earth.'"

ASH-WEDNESDAY.

"Remember, man, that thou are dust
  And shalt to dust return :"—
Then place not in the world thy trust,
  Its joys delusive spurn ;
Prepare thee for the mighty change
  Impending over all ;
Give to thy thoughts a loftier range—
  List to thy heavenward call.

The days on which mankind record
  The Saviour's birth are gone :
Behold He comes to preach the word :
  His humbler life is done.
For thirty years he show'd the humble how to
    live :—
Mark how he arm'd Himself against the world
    to strive.

He turn'd Him from the Jordan side,
And sought the lonely desert wide :
There communed with Himself and God ;
Chastised Himself, nor tasted food ;
There overcame the tempter : there
  Prepared for his high ministry
By fasting, solitude, and prayer ;—
  Then went to teach the world and die.

This would He have his followers spurn
  The pride of life, and thus prepare
To obey the call of heaven, and learn
  The grace of heaven itself to share.
Shall we, the world has long beguiled,
  Refuse to fast, refuse to fly ?
Shall we with hearts and souls defiled
  By earth and earth's iniquity,
The fruit of all his sufferings implore,
Yet, guilty, scorn to bear, what innocent He
    bore ?

No : let us hail the words that now
Warn us against life's fleeting show,
And bid our slothful souls arise—
Prepare for nobler destinies—
Prepare far holier aims to embrace—
  And—scorning worldly hopes and pride—
Prepare, through Lent, to win the grace
  Of Easter and of Whitsuntide.
" Remember, man ! that thou art dust
  And shalt return to dust again ; "
Then let us strive, since die we must,
  To die with Christ, with Him to reign

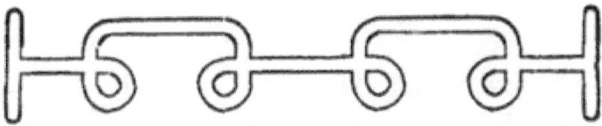

The Annunciation.[*]

All hail, Jesus! Mary, all hail!

T O-MORROW will not be a dismal day at any rate, Nina," said Marie, as they walked home from school together; "for Sister Mary Aloysia has just been telling me that the Feast of the Annunciation is, in a particular manner, 'the festival of holy hope.'"

"Yes," said Madeleine, "and Madame Margaret always told me, the very name of this feast gave her a feeling of hope and gladness whenever she pronounced it."

"Dear, dear Madame Margaret," said Marie; "it really seems a year since she died."

"And yet it is only six or seven weeks at the most, Marie."

"I will bring some violets to her grave

[*] Continued from "Ash-Wednesday."

to-morrow," said Nina; "she loved them so much, the violets of March!"

"And I will bring some primroses," said Marie. "Do let us get all the flowers we can, Madeleine, and make her grave quite beautiful for her favourite feast."

Madeleine willingly consented to this plan; and after the early Mass next morning, they all met together round the little mound of turf which covered the mortal remains of their good old friend.

"Now let us arrange our flowers, Madeleine. We have got blue-bells, and daffodils, and wild sorrel, and almond blossoms; but most primroses and blue violets, I think."

"I do not know how it is," said little Nina, after they had worked for some time in silence, "but this feast always does make me think of primroses."

"And of violets," added Madeleine; "Madame Margaret used always to say, she kept it in the primrose and violet corner of her imagination."

"I suppose because it comes in the season of the violets," said Marie.

"Perhaps that had something to say to it but she had another reason also, though I can not remember what it was. Dear Madame Margaret, how I wish she was here to tell it to us herself!"

"What is it you wish Madame Margaret to tell you?" said a sweet low voice at her elbow.

Nina and Marie both screamed at this unexpected interruption; and when Madeleine turned round, she saw a lady standing at the foot of the grave, with her eyes fixed on the name of Margaret, now written in flowery letters on the turf; she was very pale, and there was a loving sweetness in her eyes: they looked as if they had grown calm through excess of weeping.

"Madame Margaret is dead," stammered Madeleine, "and this is her grave."

"Well, then," said the lady, with a smile that won the children's hearts in a moment, "perhaps I can answer your question, if you will only tell me what it is you wish to know."

"Oh," said Madeleine, blushing, "I dare say it was only nonsense after all; but I wanted to know why the Feast of the Annunciation always puts one in mind of the spring flowers ?"

"I do not think it is such nonsense," said the lady, smiling; "the beautiful things of nature would become twice as beautiful to us, if we learned to associate them in our minds with the beauty and goodness of Him who made them ; and the meanest and apparently most useless weed that grows, has doubtless fulfilled the intention of its Creator, when it lifts our souls from earth to heaven."

"The spring flowers always do put me in mind of Mary, certainly," said Marie thoughtfully ; "but I wish you would tell me why."

"Perhaps it is because they are the promise of something better which is to come. When the angel announced to Mary that she was chosen to be the mother of God, he must have looked upon her, as we look upon a sweet spring flower, which tells us that summer is at hand, and that winter is passing away."

"I remember now what Madame Margaret said," cried Madeleine ; "sin was the spiritual winter of the world, and Mary was its spring, through whom we receive Jesus Christ, the

true summer of the children of God. But it
was the *mystery* of the Annunciation which
put her so much in mind of the violet."

"That I can easily understand," the lady
answered; "the violet hides itself beneath its
leaves, and we only discover it by its rich per-
fume. And the mystery of the Incarnation of
Jesus Christ, which we celebrate on the Feast
of the Annunciation, was accomplished in se-
cret and in silence, beneath the humble roof
of an humble virgin, and was only made known
by the sweet tidings of salvation which it shed
over the world."

"I wish you would tell us something more
about it," said Marie; "you speak very like
Madame Margaret."

The lady paused a moment, and then she
stooped to the grave and took up a bunch of
lilies of the valley, which she mingled with
some violets. "Look," said she; "if I had a
chapel dedicated to Mary, it is with these
flowers alone I would adorn the altars on her
own dear festival of 'Lady-day.' The lily of
purity, the violet of humility; Mary was so
pure, that she would nct consent to become

the mother of God, until the angel had assured her she should still remain a virgin; and so humble, that instead of taking to herself (as she well might have done) the title of His mother, she only styled herself the handmaid of the Lord. The history of this feast appears to me the best of all possible lessons for little maidens like yourselves," continued the lady, affectionately folding the children's hands within her own. "The angel Gabriel found Mary, not in the streets, not in the public places, but in the solitude of her own chamber, probably engaged in prayer, since it is in prayer that God visits us most abundantly with His graces; he saluted her with reverence, as the future mother of Jesus, and, instead of being delighted by his praise, she considered in silence, and with a modest blush upon her countenance, what he could intend by such flattering expressions. May you take this lesson to your inmost hearts, my children, and when you are addressed in words of flattery, may you ask yourselves, with Mary, what they can possibly mean? Remember that she who thus pause' in doubt was about to become the

mother of God, and the words which had trou-
bled her were the words of an angel; while
you are but creatures subject to sin, and those
who would flatter you perhaps even more sin-
ful than yourselves."

"But though Mary did not like to be praised
even by an angel," said little Marie, "still she
must have known that she was the most perfect of God's creatures, since He had chosen
her to become the mother of His Son."

"Mary did not know this, my child, when
the angel first stood before her, and said, 'Hail,
full of grace, the Lord is with thee; blessed
art thou among women;' and supposing she
had known it, she also knew that all the virtues
with which she was adorned were entirely the
gifts of her heavenly Father, who had made
her more fair and sinless than the very angels,
in order that she might become a more fitting
temple for the habitation of His divine Son.
In her deep humility, she clearly saw a truth
we often find it difficult to discover; which is,
that as God made us out of nothing, so He
alone ought to be glorified for any good quality
we may possess; therefore, when St. Elizabeth

astonished at the great honour conferred upon Mary, cried out, 'And whence is this to me, that the mother of my Lord should come unto me?' she only answered, giving all the glory to God, 'My soul doth magnify the Lord, and my spirit hath rejoiced in God my Saviour.'"

"I confess," said Madeleine, "I sometimes feel vain because people praise me for being good, and because Father Pierre once said I was the best girl in the village."

"But *why* are you good?" asked the lady with a smile; "can you tell me *what* makes you good?"

"I can hardly say," said Madeleine, colouring; "but I believe it is because I want so very much to become good, and therefore I do not like to do bad things, which I know would prevent my being so."

"But who made you want so very much to be good, my child? Can you tell me that?"

"I am sure I don't know," said Madeleine; "but I am always thinking of it, though I cannot say exactly what puts it into my head."

"My dear child, do you not perceive that it is God Himself who sends you this wish to be good, and who gives you the grace to be what you wish? We are of our own nature so much inclined to evil, we should do it continually, were it not for this good will, which is the pure gift of His infinite mercy towards us."

"I see," said Madeleine; "and I will try and remember this whenever I am tempted to feel vain again. Will you be so kind as to tell us who first established this feast in the Church?"

"I cannot tell you, my dear; but I know it is mentioned by a writer of the fifth century, and was probably celebrated by the Christians of the primitive Church long before that period. Many learned authors think that Mary herself was the first to observe this festival, and that the Apostles afterwards kept it in devout imitation of the mother of their divine Lord."

"I dare say the blessed Virgin did observe it with great devotion," answered Madeleine "for we always keep in memory the anniversary of our first communion; and I suppose, as Jesus came to her for the first time that day, it was to her what a first communion day is to us."

"Happy the child," replied the lady, "who

meets her God for the first time with something of the feelings with which Mary received Him. She was so pure, so humble, so rapt in deep devotion; Jesus was all the world to her; and all the world was nothing to her without Jesus. Would indeed that we could feel this, in some degree at least, as she did."

"Madame Margaret used often to talk to me about this mystery while I was preparing for my first communion," said Madeleine; "and when I went into my retreat three days before the Feast of Corpus Christi, she desired me to consider well the life which Mary led at Nazareth before the visit of the angel, and to endeavour to copy it as far as I could."

"She was very right," said the lady; "a great desire to receive Jesus in the disposition with which Mary received Him, would be the best of all possible preparations for receiving Him well."

"She said," continued Madeleine, "that the life of Mary at this period was one which any young girl could try and imitate, even without going into a retreat."

"Yes," said the lady "it was so simple, it

consisted so entirely in doing common things *uncommonly* well. The young girl who would imitate Mary has only to perform her daily duties with a little more exactness than she would otherwise have done. To rise, for example, at the instant she is called, without indulging for a minute in the laziness of a first awaking; to withdraw her mind a little more completely from worldly thoughts while she is in prayer; to be a little more temperate at her meals, a little more slow to speak, a little more industrious to work; these were the virtues of Mary; and the more closely we try to approach her in such *little* things, the more perfectly shall it be given to us to resemble her afterwards in the rapturous welcome which she gave to Jesus."

"That was just the way Madame Margaret used to talk about it," said Madeleine, looking quite delighted; "and she also told me, that though the purity of our heavenly mother was far above all human comprehension, I ought yet to try and approach it, as nearly as I could, by making a general confession of all the sins of my past life; and when I had once done this, she said I might remain in great peace, and expect with Mary the coming of my God."

" Did she tell you any thing more ?" asked her listener, who seemed interested by Madeleine's eager detail.

" Not exactly about our blessed Mother," answered Madeleine; " but I remember her telling me, as a preparation for communion, to consider in what manner I should welcome Jesus, if He were still living upon earth, and had sent me word He was coming to see me. In the first place, she said, she supposed I would have my house perfectly clean, and this was to be done by a good and humble confession; then she thought I would try and make the chamber in which I was to bring Him more bright and cheerful, by filling it with flowers, and opening the window to the sunshine. The flowers of the heart, she said, must consist in good actions and fervent aspirations of the soul to God; and the sunshine could only be procured by loving confidence in Him who was the true joy and sunshine of the human heart."

" Well, and what came next, Madeleine ?" asked Marie.

"Why then she told me to imagine that some one came to tell me He was at the door. How eagerly I would run to meet Him; how devoutly I would prostrate myself to receive His blessing; and when I had conducted Him into my chamber, how I would seat myself at His feet, not speaking to Him, nor yet even asking Him to speak to me, but tasting in silence the sweetness of His divine presence."

"I used to like her to talk in this way," continued Madeleine, "because it made it all so very, very real to me. I knew very well before that I should really receive Jesus in the blessed Sacrament; but I did not know how entirely we might learn to feel that He was looking at us, listening to us, loving us, and inviting us to love Him, and to let Him fold us to His bosom."

"There is Annette coming towards us," cried Nina, suddenly interrupting her sister; "how I should like to be with her running after the sheep!"

"Do not go just yet," said the lady; "I want to tell you a story of a child, who was not much older, though I am afraid a great deal wiser than you are, my little one," she added, patting Nina kindly on the head. The little girl sat down directly; and both Marie and Madeleine drew closer to the lady as she began her story.

"Once upon a time, you must know, my children, there lived a lady on the top of a hill, and this hill was surrounded by an immense forest, which she had to pass whenever she wished to ride into the country beyond. This was often the case, for the lady was a bold huntress, and she and her merry friends soon filled the whole land with the fame of their great deeds in the chase. One night she and her train were returning late from the hunt, and at first they were in high glee, and full of fun and laughter; but by degrees a kind of sadness seemed to steal over them all. One voice died away after another, until at last they paced along in utter silence. It was so dark, they could only just distinguish the branches of the trees, as they waved in the night air over their heads, and the tramping of their horses hoofs was the only sound that broke the stillness of the forest. 'It is the eve of Lady-day,

said one of the party at last, and no one knew
why he had made the remark, for their thoughts
had not been with God or our Lady during the
live-long day. Lady Ellen sighed; when she
was younger she had never failed to gather
flowers for the festivals of Mary; but this time
all had been forgotten in the pleasure of the
chase, and the Lady Chapel at the castle was
in darkness, and unadorned for the beautiful
day which had brought salvation into the
world. 'I will hunt no more,' she said to herself, 'since it has made me forget what I owe
to the Mother of God.' Just then a soft strain
of music seemed to float along the air, and a
light rose up from the depths of the forest;
and it grew, and grew, and grew, in intensity
and brightness, until you could have found the
smallest weed only by its lustre; it was softer
than the sun, brighter than the moon, and it
seemed to concentrate itself in one spot, where
all the party knew an old oak-tree had stood
in the morning; but they could not see it now,
the strange light so dazzled their eyes. 'Who
will follow me?' cried Lady Ellen, springing
without assistance from her palfrey. No one

offered to stir; but Lady Ellen was brave, and
except her too great passion for hunting there
was no fault in her; so she signed herself with
the sign of the cross, and boldly advanced towards the wonderful light.   It grew brighter
and brighter as she came closer, and then it
seemed to float away on either side, while a
stream of rich music issued from its centre.
Ellen now saw that she was standing close to
the oak-tree, and that a little child was lying
at her feet.   'Poor little thing,' thought Lady
Ellen, 'doubtless its cruel parents have left it
in this forest, and our good Mother in heaven
would not see it perish without baptism, but
sent the great light we saw to guide me to the
spot, in order to save it.'   Saying this, she lifted
the infant from the ground, and folded it to her
bosom; and while she did so, she thought of
the love of Jesus for His little ones on earth,
and a voice seemed to say in her ear, 'He that
receiveth one such little child in My name receiveth Me.'   Lady Ellen returned slowly to the
castle, amid many holy thoughts and good res-
olutions; and going straight to the chapel, she
found it lit up with a number of candles, and

the old priest waiting at the door to receive her.

"'Where is the child?' said he, as soon as ever he perceived her coming.

"'But how did you know there was a child?' she asked, in great amazement.

"'Not half an hour ago,' he answered, 'a lady dressed in white told me to have all things prepared to give holy baptism to a child whom you had found in the forest. She said he should be a great saint, and should be called Bonaventure; and that in return for the charity you had shown him, he should one day be the means of procuring you a great treasure.' Lady Ellen held the infant at the baptismal font that night; and the next morning she assembled all her thoughtless companions, and told them that, as she intended to spend the rest of her days entirely in the service of God, the castle would doubtless be too dull an abode for them; she therefore advised them to go and seek for amusement elsewhere, unless indeed they chose to follow her example, and share in her exer cises of devotion. Some laughed, some admired her resolution, but none had courage enough to

renounce the world with her; so they presently
all went away, and she was left alone with the
infant she had adopted. From that hour she
became an altered being; she employed her
time in reading, praying, serving the sick and
poor, and, above all the rest, in instructing the
little Bonaventure, who grew up so good and
wise that, before he reached his seventh year,
he was known throughout the country by no
other name than that of the Little Saint. To
adorn the Lady Chapel was the chief delight
both of Ellen and the child; and while she sat
at home and spun fine linen for the altar, he
wandered forth through wood and field in
search of flowers to place upon it; winter and
summer, fair weather or foul, ever on the eve
of the festivals of Mary, he sallied out with his
little basket in his hand, and never did he bring
it back unfilled; so that people used to say our
Lady herself must provide him with flowers,
since he found them even in the season when
nature had none to offer. Six times had Lady-
day passed over his head since his first arrival
at the castle, and on the eve of the seventh he
went as usual to seek flowers for the altar of

his *mother ;* for so he ever called our Lady,
and he used to name her with such a look of
love and hope, as any other child might have
worn when it spoke of an earthly parent. He
took the path leading towards the old oak-tree,
and there, by the soft light which ever seemed
to hang like a mist above it, he saw some little
lambs, as fair as snow, standing around a circle
of white sweet violets. Perhaps Bonaventure
was used to strange sights, for he knelt down
quietly, and began to fill his basket with the
flowers, when lo! they vanished all away, and
a sweet low voice seemed to say in his ear, 'an
image of our dear Lady lies buried here. More
innocent than the lambs of the field, more full
of virtue than the violet is of fragrance, must
he be who is to bear it from this spot.'

"Then went back the child to Ellen, and he
told her of the wondrous image, and of the
holiness of him who was to find it in the forest.
And Lady Ellen sought a hermit, the holiest
man in all the country round, and bade him
bring it from the old oak-tree. But no lambs
or violets could he discover there; and a voice,
as of sorrow murmured in his ear, 'Hermit,

go back; thou hast mingled blood with the
waters of baptism, and Mary will not let thee
see; for charity is the cherished virtue of those
who love her.' The hermit wept at Ellen's
feet, and said, 'In my youth I slew a brother,
so Mary will not let me see; for charity is the
cherished virtue of those who love her.' And
Lady Ellen next besought a priest, that he
would bear the image from the forest. But
neither flower nor lambkin greeted his approach; and a voice of warning said in his ear,
'Priest, go back; pride hath darkened over thy
soul, and Mary will not let thee see; for humility is the fairest jewel in the crown of those
who love her.' The priest returned, and said,
with many a sigh, 'I thought, in my pride, I
was better than the hermit, guilty of his brother's blood; therefore Mary will not let me see;
for humility is the fairest jewel in the crown
of those who love her.' And Lady Ellen asked
a nun to seek the image at the old oak-tree.
But lambs and violets vanished as she came;
and a voice of anger thundered in her ear,
  Unfaithful one, go back; thy thoughts have
not been always of angel whiteness, and Mary

will not let thee see; for those who truly love her, wrap their souls in purity, as in a garment.'

"The spouse of the crucified Saviour wept in shame and grief as she said to Ellen, 'My thoughts have not been always of angel whiteness, therefore Mary will not let me see; for those who truly love her, wrap their souls in purity, as in a garment.' And Lady Ellen wrung her hands, as she cried aloud, 'Where, then, shall I find one who is meek and pure and lowly, with the dews of baptism yet bright on the soul?' And then she thought upon the little child;—so simple, innocent, and free from guile. And she said to him, 'Haste thee, haste thee, little child, and bring thy mother's image from the old oak-tree.'

"But the child hung back, and said, 'Send me not to seek that holy image. I am but a simple little child, and unworthy of so high a task;' and the Lady Ellen answered,

"'Thou art indeed a very simple little child; but thou art humble, pure, and meek; and Mary loves the little ones who resemble thee.

"And the child went forth once more to the old oak-tree. And the violets were sweet, and the lambs were fair, and the image lay on the turf beside them; and he bore it in safety to the Lady Ellen. Full soon there rose a stately church on the place where the oak-tree grew before, and the image was placed within it; and night and day were holy monks who watched before it. Then the Lady Ellen left her castle, and sought repose within the shadows of the cloister; but never would the boy depart from that lonely forest. He built himself a hermitage, and ever he prayed before the image of our Lady, that she would keep him lowly in his own esteem, pure and simple as a little child. And so he lived, and so he died. His form grew bent, and his hair became white with age, but still in heart a very child was he; *most* dear to Christ and our Lady ever blessed. Therefore did she stand beside him in his dying hour, and bear his soul to Paradise in her bosom; while the monks, they buried his body at the very gates of the Lady Church, where his life had been spent in watching and in prayer."

"It would have been no use his being a little child, if he had not also been good; he

would not have found the image, would he ?"
asked Marie, as soon as the lady had finished
her story.

"Surely not, my dear. If he had been a
proud, peevish, or disobedient child, he would
not have been innocent and dear to Mary."

"There is Annette and her flock of sheep!"
cried Nina. "Look, Marie! one of them has
tumbled into the pool below; and it will certainly be drowned."

"Poor Annette!" cried Marie; "her master
will beat her, if that is the case. Let us go
and try to help her."

"We must make haste, then," said Nina;
and away the children flew down the hill,
heedless of Madeleine's warning voice to take
care; for the pool was very deep.

Marie arrived first, and found Annette standing at the very edge of the water, holding a
long stick with a crook at the end of it towards
the drowning lamb; while the poor mother
sheep anxiously watched her operations in
favour of her little one, and bleated most
piteously all the time. Without a moment's
thought, the little girl jumped into the water

and seized the lamb; the next instant she was out of her depth, and felt herself sinking. "Catch hold of the stick! catch hold of the stick!" cried Annette, in great alarm. Marie tried to reach it, but the lamb struggled in her arms, and she would not let it go.

"Let go the lamb! let go the lamb! or you will be drowned," shouted Annette and Nina, both together, as loud as they could. By this time Madeleine, wild with terror, came running to the spot, but, almost before she knew what was really the matter, the lady had stepped into the water, and, as it was not much higher than her waist, she easily succeeded in bringing Marie and the lamb safe to land. It was a fine but rather sharp day, and both Marie and her little prize shivered, as much perhaps from fear as cold; and the lady looked kindly at the little pale face, and the blue fingers still clasped tightly round the lamb.

"You had better take her home and change her things as quickly as you can," she said to Madeleine.

In obedience to this order, Marie gave the lamb into Annette's care, and then, after a mo ment's blushing hesitation, she knelt down and kissed the hand of her kind deliverer.

"Which is the shortest way to the castle on the hill?" asked the lady; "is it not through the village?"

"Yes," said both Nina and Annette, in a tone of great astonishment. For the castle on the hill belonged to the Countess Drisbach— the great lady of the village, which had lately been thrown into a state of much excitement by the unexpected tidings that she was coming to reside there. She had spent all the early part of her life in Italy, so that she was not personally known to any of the children.

"Well, then," said the lady, "I will walk with you part of the way. Marie, my child, you are very fond of lambs, I suppose, since you risk your life so readily for one."

"Yes, madame," answered Marie; "I love little lambs dearly, they put me in mind of Jesus, who was also called a lamb; but I did not remember that when I jumped into the water; I was only thinking of poor Annette; for the master would beat her," she added in a low voice, "if any of the lambs were missing."

" My poor little child !" said the lady, in a
tone full of compassion ; "do you mean to say
your master would really beat you if the lamb
were drowned ?"

" Why not ?" said Annette, rather in a sulky
tone.   " It would have been all my own fault.
If I had been minding my business, instead of
wondering what you were all doing at Madame
Margaret's grave, the lamb could not have got
away as it did."

The lady smiled.   " Who is this little girl's
master ?" she asked of Madeleine.

" His name is Pippo, and he is one of the
Countess Drisbach's shepherds.   But he is a
hard man, and not very kind to poor little
Annette," Madeleine answered, with a glance
of compassion at the young shepherdess.

" Then it is one of my lambs you have
saved," said the Countess to Marie ; "and from
this moment it is your own, as a reward for
your kindness in trying to save Annette a
beating."

" Mine ?" cried Marie, in a tone of joyful sur
prise.   " Oh, how glad I am ! the dear little
creature ! pray give it to me directly," said she,

trying to take it out of Annette's arms. But this the little shepherdess stoutly resisted.

"Not so fast, Madame Marie! You *were* very kind to me, it is true; and I *am* very much obliged to you; but for all that, you cannot have the lamb just yet."

"And why cannot she have the lamb?" asked the Countess, in a tone of displeased surprise. "It is mine, and I have given it to her. Surely I have a right to do what I like with my own."

"And pray, how am I to know that it is your own?" Annette answered still more rudely.

"How?" said the lady, "why, did I not tell you I was the Countess Drisbach?"

"So you say," the little shepherdess returned; "but, for any thing I know to the contrary, you may be only pretending to be her, in order to rob me of the lamb; and as far as Master Pippo is concerned, it will be all the same to poor Annette, whether the creature was drowned or stolen."

"Good gracious!" cried Madeleine; "how cross you are, Annette! how can you speak so rudely to the lady?"

"Never mind," said the Countess, laughing

" Annette is a little rude, certainly ; but she is
quite right not to give up the lamb without
knowing for certain that it is mine to dispose of.
However, do you, my little girl, bring it up to
the castle this evening ; and I think I shall be
able to convince you I am really the Countess,
and tell your master to come likewise."

" Yes, madame," said Annette more civilly,
dropping a curtsy, and then turning into a path
which led towards the shepherd's cottage.

" That child has been harshly treated,"
thought the Countess, as she pursued her way
with the other children ; and she remained absorbed in thought, until she heard Marie say
to her sister, " Madeleine, is it not the Countess
Drisbach that our old pilgrim is for ever talking about ?"

" Yes, Nina ; I was just thinking about it
when you spoke."

" Did you speak about a pilgrim, my child ?"
asked the Countess hurriedly.

" Yes, madame," cried Nina, joyfully, " a real
pilgrim—all the way from the Holy Land, and
he always is asking about you. He says you
bade him wait here your arrival at the castle."

"Then it *is* the same," murmured the Countess in a low voice, as she took leave of the little party at the entrance of the village.

The children all supped together that night; and it would be almost impossible to say how often they ran to the door, or looked out of the window, in expectation of the arrival of the little shepherdess. She came at last, and with a face more radiant than any one had ever seen it before; she placed the lamb in Marie's lap, crying out at the same time, "It was the real Countess, after all; and she sends you the lamb, and look what she gave to me!" and Annette held up a piece of silver, which glittered bright in the light of the fire; "she gave it me, all for myself; and, what is better still," added the poor little shepherdess, sidling up to Marie, "she told Master Pippo not to beat me any more. She said he should not be her shepherd if he did so again."

"Poor child!" said the pilgrim in a tone of compassion; "then I trust we shall never see you again with those black and blue marks on your poor little neck and shoulders."

"Thank you, Master Pilgrim," said the

child gratefully; "and that puts me in mind
the lady wishes to see you this very night."

"This very night!" echoed the old man.
"But if she wish it, I must go, and the sooner
it is over, the better."

He took his staff, and sallied out as he mut-
tered these words, leaving the farmer and his
family in some surprise.   An hour afterwards,
when he returned, his face was pale and hag-
gard, and his eyes looked red with weeping.

"Have you seen the Countess?" the children all asked the moment his foot had touched
the threshold.

"I have seen an angel!" he answered, sinking down on a chair, and burying his face in
both his hands.

"An angel!" cried Nina.   "She is the
Countess of Drisbach.   She is not an angel."

"Well," replied Marie; "I think Master
Pilgrim is right.   I am sure she looked just
like an angel this morning when she was telling us all those pretty things about the Feast
of the Annunciation."

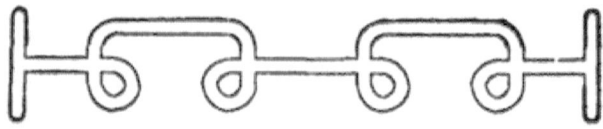

Holy Week.*

All hail, Jesus! Mary, all hail!

I LIKE my palm-branch much better than yours, Madeleine," said Nina to her sister, as they left church together on Palm Sunday,—" look, it is laurel, tied up with some nice delicate young sprigs of the box-tree."

"And I like mine the best," said Madeleine, laughing; "I love the saltow, with its soft mouse-like buds of green; it seems so fresh and full of spring."

"The pilgrim has got a real palm, which he brought all the way from Jerusalem," said Marie.

"A real palm!—oh, let us go and ask him to show it to us directly," cried Nina; and away she flew after the pilgrim, whom she

* Continued from the "Festival of the Annunciation."

overtoook just as he reached the farmer's cottage. "If you please, sir," she said, all out of breath from her race, "will you show us your real palm, and tell us how you got it, and all about it?"

"Very willingly," said the pilgrim, who was a great favourite with all the children; and in a few minutes he placed it in Nina's eager hands.

"It is not pretty at all," she said, in a tone of disappointment, handing it to her sister and Marie.

"It is faded now," he answered, with a sigh; "it was a magnificent branch when I received it from the hands of the father guardian of the Franciscan convent at Jerusalem."

"Did you not receive it in the church, then?" asked Nina.

"I received it in the church of the Holy Sepulchre, which is built not only over the tomb of Jesus, but also over the place on Mount Calvary where He was crucified."

"And did you really, *really* see the very spot where Jesus was laid in the sepulchre?" said Marie, in a tone of doubting wonder.

"These eyes have seen it, these lips have

touched it," he answered in a voice of deep emotion ; " the tomb is cut in the living rock, and is enclosed in a small chapel, where a Franciscan priest says Mass every morning on a portable altar, which is afterwards removed ; upon Palm Sunday, however, there was a temporary altar erected outside the Holy Sepulchre, and here the father guardian of the Franciscans blessed the palms, whole forests of which were piled around it, and afterwards distributed them among the pilgrims and the rest of the faithful, having first taken one left on purpose for himself, and adorned with flowers so entwined as to form a pontifical crown at the top. The procession then set out, and made the round of the Holy Sepulchre three times in the most perfect order and recollection."

" In our village," said Nina, " the procession is *outside* the church ; and then some of the choir go inside and shut the doors, and sing a hymn ; and then the choir on the outside answer them, and then the sub-deacon strikes the doors with the end of the cross, and then they are opened, and we all go in with our palms in our hands."

"Those within the church," answered the pilgrim, "represent the choirs of heavenly spirits, and those without, the faithful upon earth joining their voices together in praise of the triumphs of Christ their King; and the doors of the church open when they are struck with the staff of the cross the deacon carries in his hand, in order to show us that Christ, by dying on the cross, conquered sin, which is the real gate that closes the entrance of heaven against us."

"But I thought we received palms in memory of the palm and olive-branches which the Hebrews carried before Jesus at His entrance into Jerusalem?" said Madeleine.

"So we do," answered the pilgrim; "but they are also emblems of the crowns we shall hereafter receive in reward of our good works, and victories over our temptations to sin. I should have told you that, formerly, in order to imitate more perfectly the entrance of Christ into Jerusalem, the father guardian used to go on Palm Sunday to the village of Bethphage; two of his religious then brought him an ass, upon which they had spread their mantles, and as soon as the father was mounted, they led him into the city by the very gate through which Jesus Himself had entered, all the faithful going before, and strewing the road with olive-leaves and flowers, and shouting, as the children of Israel formerly did, 'Hosanna! blessed is he that cometh in the name of the Lord,—Hosanna in the highest!' This public procession, however, no longer takes place, in consequence of the difficulty of obtaining leave for it from the Turkish government."

"It must have been a very solemn feeling to follow the ceremonies of Holy Week in the very church of the Holy Sepulchre," observed Minette, who had now joined, as she often did, the circle round the pilgrim.

"It was both sweet and solemn," he returned, "to listen to the Passion chanted over the very tomb of the Saviour, to hear *His own* words in the very city where they were formerly spoken, to follow Him step by step through the Via Dolorosa—the way of sorrow—the street of tears, as it has been sometimes called, from the place where He first received the cross upon His mangled shoulders, to that

where He sank beneath its terrible burden.—
No! never can I make you understand what
I felt when the guide stopped me, and said,
'This is the spot where Jesus first met His
holy Mother.'"

"But the ceremonies themselves of Holy
Week are the same at Jerusalem as they are
every where else, are they not?" asked Madeleine.

"Certainly; but I think it would be difficult
to *feel* them any where else exactly in the same
manner as one does at Jerusalem; for there the
stations of the Passion are made on the very
places where they formerly occurred; thus, on
Wednesday in Holy Week, the Father Franciscans make a station, and say many Masses,
in the very grotto where Jesus sweat blood,
and suffered Himself to be consoled by an
angel."

"I always thought His agony took place in
the garden of Gethsemane," said Minette.

"The grotto is in the garden, and it is in
the very same state in which it was when
Jesus prayed there with a soul sorrowful even
unto death--less at the prospect of His own

sufferings than of our crimes and ingratitude
for whom they were to be endured."

"And did you also make a station in the
grotto of the agony?" asked Marie.

"I went there with the Franciscan Fathers,
and I afterwards followed them to the church
of the Holy Sepulchre, where they chanted
Tenebræ."

"I never can remember that word," said
Nina, "It is so difficult, and it seems to have
no meaning."

"It has a meaning, however," returned the
pilgrim, "and perhaps you will remember it
better, when I tell you that it comes from a
Latin word which signifies *darkness*."

"But Tenebræ is said in broad day-light,"
persisted Nina.

"But in the early ages," answered the old
man, "the Christians used to spend the greater
part of the nights of Holy Week watching in
the churches, and this office was then said at
midnight; it received its name partly for this
reason, and partly perhaps because of the
gradually extinguishing of the lights which
takes place during the service."

"I have often wondered," said Madeleine, "what was the meaning of that triangular candlestick with fifteen candles, seven on each side, and one on the top, which is the only one left burning, and even that is hid for a time behind the altar."

"The fourteen candles are commonly supposed to represent the Apostles (who were called by our Saviour the light of the world), our blessed Lady, and the rest of the holy women ; and their extinction is emblematic of their flight or mourning at the death of Jesus ; but the candle at the top is supposed to represent Christ Himself; it is therefore only concealed for a time behind the altar, and is brought forth again, in order to show us that He was only hid for a little while in the sepulchre, after which He rose again to life ; for this reason the top candle is always made of white wax, while the others are generally of common or yellow, such as the Church prescribes to be used in times of penance or of mourning."

"The Tenebræ is always said on the wrong day," said Nina; "Wednesday for Thursday

—Thursday for Friday—Friday for Saturday
—what is the reason of that, I wonder ?"

"I have told you these prayers were formerly
said at midnight; and when such nightly as-
semblies were no longer held, the Church gave
permission for the Tenebræ being chanted on
the evening before. If you read the Psalms
and Lessons attentively, you will find that those
meant for Thursday lead us in a particular manner to consider the preparations for the Passion
of Jesus Christ, both in the cenacle and the
Garden of Olives ; those for Friday recall to
our minds His passion and death ; and those
for Saturday the mysteries of His burial and
descent into hell."

"That is, I suppose," said Madeleine, "because on Maunday Thursday the Church cele-
brates the institution of the Blessed Sacrament; on Good Friday, the death of Jesus on
the cross ; on Holy Saturday, His being laid
in the sepulchre."

"And the Lamentations," said Minette,
"they are so sad and beautiful, and move one
to tears one scarce knows why,—they are
from the prophet Jeremiah, are they not ?"

" In those sad strains," returned the pilgrim, " the prophet mourned over the ruin of Jerusalem, and the captivity of her people ; and this is but a very imperfect image of the deplorable slavery to which mankind was reduced by sin, before the Passion and Death of Jesus ; weep, therefore, when you hear them ; weep for your own sins and for those of the world ; God and His angels only know how terrible is the state of a soul in mortal sin. Well might such a one cry out with the prophet, ' The mercies of the Lord, that we are not consumed, because His tender mercies have not failed.' "

The pilgrim hid his face in his hands as he spoke, and there was a long and awful pause, which Nina broke at last by asking him, where they placed the Blessed Sacrament on Maunday Thursday after Mass at Jerusalem ? " Madeleine tells me," she added, " that here they bear it to an altar which is called the Sepulchre, and which is adorned with flowers and lace, and even precious stones, when they can get them."

" It is not so beautiful perhaps at Jerusalem.

my child, but it is certainly more awful; for after Mass the Blessed Sacrament is borne in solemn procession three times round the little chapel of the Holy Sepulchre, which is splendidly illuminated with lamps and tapers; it is then deposited in a silver tabernacle on the very tomb of Jesus; and the Franciscan Fathers keep watch before it night and day, two at a time, who, after an hour's adoration, are replaced by two more. The vestments used that day were of black velvet, embroidered in gold, the most magnificent, I think, that I have ever seen."

"I thought the vestments were always white upon Maunday Thursday," observed Madeleine.

"In most places the vestments are white on Maunday Thursday, in order to testify the joy and gratitude of the Church for the institution of the Blessed Sacrament; at Jerusalem, however, it is otherwise, and perhaps during the three last days of Holy Week any thing denoting joy would be inadmissible in that city, over which Jesus wept, in which He suffered, and by which He died."

"Madame Drisbach told me the other day," said Madeleine, "that on Maunday Thursday the Pope washes the feet of thirteen poor priests, and afterwards waits on them at table, in commemoration of our Blessed Saviour's washing His disciples' feet before the last supper; and she says that it is also the custom for people of the highest rank to go to the hospitals to wash and dress the galled feet of the poor pilgrims, who come from all parts of the world to spend Holy Week at Rome."

"The ladies go the hospital for women pilgrims," added Nina, "and the princes and noblemen to that intended for men."

"Yes," answered the old man; "and they do this act of charity with a kindness and simplicity which make the poor pilgrims feel that they are indeed performing it as a service of love. In the old Catholic times kings and queens thought themselves honoured by imitating this humble action of the humble Jesus; and I have read somewhere or other an interesting account of the holy St. Elizabeth, who, on Maunday Thursday, always put aside all that could remind her she was the daughter of the King of Hungary, and dressing herself in mean clothes, with only sandals on her feet,

washed the feet of twelve poor men, some
times lepers, giving to each twelve pieces of
money, a loaf of bread, and a white dress."

"But, if you please," asked Marie, "will
you tell me *why* the Blessed Sacrament is
taken from the high altar and placed in a
sepulchre? I don't quite understand the
reason of this change."

"There is no Host consecrated on Good
Friday," answered the pilgrim; "but during
the Mass of Maunday Thursday the priest consecrates two, one of which he receives, and the
other he places on an altar prepared for this
purpose; on Good Friday he bears it back
again to the high altar, where he consumes it
during the Mass, which, for this reason, is
called the Mass of the Pre-sanctified, or of the
Host consecrated the day before."

"But what is the reason the priest does not
consecrate upon Good Friday?" Madeleine
now asked.

"I do not know exactly the time in which
the Mass of the Pre-sanctified was first intro-
duced—perhaps about the fifth or sixth cen
tury; but I believe that even before the fourth

century it was the custom to omit Mass altogether both on Good Friday and Holy Saturday, in memory of the sadness of the apostles during these two days, and also in sign of the mourning of the Church for the death of her divine spouse, Jesus."

" I remember, when I was a child, I used to feel quite frightened on entering the church on Good Friday," said Minette ; " the altar always looked so dismal, stript of its ornaments, and with the door of the tabernacle flung wide open. I used to feel inclined to fancy the priests were dead, they looked so motionless, as they lay on the steps covered with their black vestments."

" All this is meant to express the deep grief of the Church," said the pilgrim ; " and if it make us feel dismal, it is in some degree the effect which she wishes it to produce in our souls ; only while we mourn for the sufferings of our sweet Jesus, we must not forget to weep also over our own sins, by which they were caused ; and this He Himself seems to have indicated, when, turning to the women who followed Him, He bade them weep, ' not for Him but for themselves and for their children.' "

" Father Pierre told me," observed Madeleine, " that the first lesson read in the service
of Good Friday is a prophecy concerning the
mercies of Christ, and that the second is the
history of the sacrifice of the paschal lamb."

" Yes," said the pilgrim, " because the sacrifice of the paschal lamb was expressly established by God Himself among the Jewish people, as a type of the death of Jesus, who was
the true Lamb of God, without spot or stain
about Him; after these lessons, the history
of the Passion according to St. John is read;
and at its conclusion prayers are offered for all
God's creatures on the face of the earth, whether
Jews, pagans, heretics, or Christians."

" Does not the Church pray for them every
day in the Mass, then ? " asked Marie.

" Every day, in the Mass, she prays for the
salvation of the whole world; but on Good
Friday she prays for each class of persons
separately and by name; first, in order to
show us that there is no grace we may not
hope to obtain through the merits of the sacrifice of the cross; and secondly, because she
wishes, in this manner, to honour and to

imitate the immense charity of Jesus Christ, who while hanging on the cross, prayed for his most bitter enemies, exclaiming, ' Father, forgive them, for they know not what they do.' "

" We do not kneel down when we pray for the Jews," said Nina.

" No," returned the pilgrim; " and by this omission the Church would show her horror of the insult offered to Jesus by the Jews, when they bent the knee in mockery before Him. As soon as these prayers are finished, the priest uncovers the crucifix, which has been veiled in black ever since Passion Sunday, and then follows the Adoration of the Cross, during which time the choir sings the Reproaches; so called, because they are spoken in the name of Christ, who reproaches His chosen people with their ingratitude for the many blessings He has conferred upon them."

" The Adoration of the Cross," repeated Minette, with a sorrowful smile; " my poor husband used to get so angry whenever he saw that word in my Missal. I never could make him understand that we did not worship the cross."

"The word is a very old one," answered the pilgrim, "and simply meant 'veneration,' when it was first applied to the ceremony of kissing the cross. Of this there can be no doubt, since learned men tell us it was used in this sense by the early Christians at the very time when they were suffering themselves to be martyred by thousands, rather than worship the false gods of the heathens. When, therefore, Catholics speak of *adoring* the cross, they only intend to say that they honour it as the *means* of their salvation, while they keep their adoration, or supreme worship, for Him who accomplished it by dying on its arms."

"My husband used to say," observed Minette, "that the Adoration of the Cross was a modern invention of Catholics, and not a custom of the primitive Christians."

"So far from this being true," said the pilgrim, "this ceremony may be said to date from the fourth century, when the true Cross was discovered by the Empress St. Helena."

"Discovered!" said Marie, in great surprise: "why, was it ever lost, then?"

"The persecutions which directly followed

.he preaching of the Apostles, and continued
until the beginning of the fourth century,"
answered the pilgrim, " prevented the early
Christians from seeking and preserving the
relics of Christ's passion, as they otherwise
most certainly would have done. The heathens also, with a cruel ingenuity, built a temple to Venus on the very spot where he had
been buried ; so that those who came to give
the tribute of their prayers and tears to Jesus,
might appear to be performing an act of adoration to the most abominable of their false
divinities.   Perhaps you already know that
Constantine the Great, the first Christian emperor, obtained a decisive victory over his
enemies directly after the vision of a cross of
light, which appeared to him in the skies, with
the inscription round it, ' In this sign shalt thou
conquer.' When, therefore, he had obtained
peaceable possession of the imperial crown, he
was desirous of building a chuich on the very
spot where his divine Redeemer had suffered
for him ; and his mother, St. Helena, filled
with the same holy anxiety, undertook a journey to Jerusalem for this purpose in the year

of our Lord 326, and the seventy-ninth of her
age. Can you wonder that, on her arrival in
the Holy City, she became still more anxious
to discover the true cross, or that she burned,
as an old writer expresses it, with an earnest
desire of touching the remedy of immortality?
Tradition still points out the place where the
holy empress knelt in prayer while the works
necessary for this purpose were being carried
out. By her orders the temple of Venus was
thrown down, and several excavations being
made on the spot where it had stood, the Holy
Sepulchre was at last discovered, and near it
three crosses buried in the earth, as also the
inscription which had been attached to the
cross of Jesus, and the nails which had fastened His hands and feet."

"Then how did they find out which of the
three was the real cross, I wonder?" said Nina.

"The inscription, I believe, lay near one of
them," answered the pilgrim; "and the marks
where the nails had been would also serve
as an indication: however, St. Macarius, the
Bishop of Jerusalem, suggested that a miraculous proof of its identity should be asked of

God. He went, therefore, with St. Helena and other persons, to the house of a lady who lay ill in the city. The empress then said a prayer aloud, and the bishop applied the crosses one after another; the two first were without effect, but the touch of the third instantly cured the sick person, leaving no doubt in the minds of the spectators as to its being the real cross upon which Christ had suffered. Can you imagine for a moment, that St. Helena, who had made a perilous journey over sea and land for the purpose of honouring the holy places where Jesus had suffered, would not, at this discovery, have prostrated herself to kiss the cross, once stained with his precious blood; adoring, indeed, as St. Ambrose observes, ' not the wood, but the King,—Him who had hung upon the wood.' "

" Who, indeed, can doubt it for an instant ?" said Minette earnestly; "and was it at this time, then, that the adoration of the true cross began ?"

" I should say so," rejoined the pilgrim; " for St. Paulinus, who wrote in this very century, speaks of the custom of exposing the

true cross to the veneration of the faithfu
once a year, in the search of the Holy Sepulchre at Jerusalem ; and he marks the day
most clearly by saying, it is the one upon
which is celebrated the Mystery of the Cross,
that is to say, Good Friday. So, you see, nothing but ignorance could induce any one to
speak of this venerable custom as an invention
of modern Catholics."

"But the cross which we kiss is not the
true cross,—it is only a little crucifix," said
Nina.

"No," rejoined the pilgrim ; "but we kiss
this little cross in honour of the one upon
which Jesus died.   The Emperor Constantine
showed the same feeling of reverence when he
forbade the punishment of the cross, which
had formerly been the common mode of execution in the Roman empire.   He would not
have that considered dishonourable which had
been made glorious to every Christian heart
by the sufferings of Jesus ; and if you wish
for a still higher example, you will find it in
the Apostle St. Peter, who chose to be crucified with his head downwards, deeming him

self all unworthy of the death of the cross, or of dying in the same position in which the Lord of heaven and earth had suffered."

"Just one question more," said Madeleine, as she saw the pilgrim was about to withdraw; "why do we make three genuflexions when going up to kiss the cross?"

"As a reparation for the three solemn mockeries which the Jews offered to Jesus in the course of His Passion: in the house of Caiphas, where He was treated as a false prophet; at the Court of Herod, where He was regarded as a fool; and upon Mount Calvary, where He was blasphemed as an impostor. And let me advise you, dear little ones," added the pilgrim, as he paused on the threshold of the door, "at each of these genuflexions to say in your hearts some such short prayer as this; 'We adore Thee, and we bless Thee, O Jesus, because by Thy holy Cross Thou hast redeemed the world.'"

*   *   *   *   *

Father Pierre had so arranged the visits of the villagers to the Holy Sepulchre on Maunday Thursday, that the Blessed Sacrament was

never left without its adorers. He gave to
each of them a card containing the hour at
which their attendance would be required in
the church; the night-hours were assigned to
the men, and to the women those of the day
and evening. Minette's card was for the lat-
ter, because she dwelt near the church; and
it was so dark when she entered it with Marie,
that involuntarily the little girl crept closer to
her mother; but as she advanced up the aisle,
the blaze of light from the altar of the Blessed
Sacrament reassured her, and she felt as if she
were entering into the atmosphere of heaven.
Never had the Sepulchre been seen so beautifully arranged in that village before; for the
Countess had undertaken herself this labour of
love, and her magnificent diamonds were spark-
ling like dew-drops among the dark leaves of
the myrtle and the snowy bloom of the came-
lia. At first Marie's eyes would wander, in
spite of herself, to the brilliant Sepulchre, with
its flowers, its jewels, and starlike tapers; but
by degrees her thoughts seemed to calm and
settle themselves upon Him who dwelt so
lovingly within the tabernacle, trusting entirely

to His faithful people for the decoration of His
"altar-throne." She knew He loved her far
better than she could ever hope to love Him
in return, and that it was this very love which
brought Him down from heaven, where Saints
and Angels ministered to His glory, in order
to find His delight among the children of men.
She thought upon all He had done for her
during this sad and holy time of Passion-tide.
How meekly He had washed His disciples'
feet; how generously He had fed them with
His precious body and blood; how tenderly
He had suffered St. John to rest upon His
bosom; and how gently He had reproached
them in the garden when he found that they
had slept, while *He* was enduring an agony
unto blood. She thought upon Him, the
fairest and most beautiful among the sons of
men, forced through the Cedron waters by His
merciless foes, dragged from Caiphas to Pilate,
from Pilate to Herod, from Herod back again
to Pilate; now hither, now thither; now within,
now without; scourged at the pillar, crowned
with thorns, mocked, reviled, spit upon, laden
with a heavy cross, and led like an innocent

lamb to slaughter. How that cross must have pressed upon His mangled shoulders; how His tender heart must have mourned over the grief of His mother, at the very sight of whom He lost His little remaining strength, and fell beneath His burden of intolerable woe! She thought upon the nails which pierced those delicate feet, and crushed those merciful hands, so often lifted up to heaven to implore health for the sick, and peace and pardon for the penitent sinner. And while thoughts like these rushed through her mind, oh, how fervently did Marie promise never to crucify the sweet Jesus any more by wilful sin, never to wound His loving heart by want of gratitude or love towards Him! Just then she remembered that it is through Mary we must go to Jesus; so she earnestly besought this Mother of sorrows to lead her to Mount Calvary, and let her share in the grief which had pierced her own soul. Now Marie seemed indeed to be in spirit at the foot of the cross, and tears streamed down her face, as fancy painted the dying eyes of Jesus fixed lovingly on her. A low sob at last roused her from her devotions; and turning round, she

saw Annette kneeling at her side. Her hands
were also raised to heaven, her eyes were also
full of tears, and her thoughts, as the thoughts
of every Catholic child would naturally be at
such a time, were also employed in dwelling on
the sufferings of her crucified Saviour. Marie
drew closer to her; and as Minette rose to go,
she took the hand of the little shepherdess, and
led her from the church: "My poor child,"
cried Minette, when she saw her, "this is too
late an hour for you to be here."

"No, it is not," said Annette, in her usual
rough way; "master would not let me leave
the sheep to-day; but I could not go to bed
without paying a visit to Jesus in the Sepulchre. And now I must make haste home;
for I promised grandmother to be back before
a dozen stars were out in the heavens, and
there is one twinkling in the skies already."

"And will you not be at the church to-
morrow, then?" asked Marie.

"No; master will not let me come. But
look you here, Marie," continued the little shepherdess in a tone of triumph, "I have got two
·ong sticks tied in the form of a cross, and I

shall stick it up in the field, and say my beads
under it.   And Father Pierre says St. Genevieve had no better an altar than that to say
her prayers before, and yet she became a saint,
you see."

"You will be a little St. Genevieve yourself
some of these days," said Minette, laughing;
but Annette was almost out of hearing before
she had finished her speech.

Marie did think the church looked very sad
on the morning of Good Friday; but she followed the beautiful service with great interest
in a little Missal given her by the pilgrim, and
then listened very attentively to Father Pierre's
sermon.   He did not explain to his flock the
meaning of the ceremony of kissing the cross,
for this seemed as natural to them as it would
have been to have embraced the image of a
beloved father; but he spoke to them of the
glories of the cross, and of the happiness of
those who lived beneath its shadow.

He told them of the Saints who had found
in the devout contemplation of the cross the
inspiration to every high and holy action they

performed.   Of St. Thomas, who sought his
wonderful science at the foot of the crucifix;
of St. Francis, who drew from thence the
ardours of his seraphic love; of St. Augustin,
who fed his soul, as he declares, in the wounds
of Christ; of St. Bonaventure, who cried out,
in a transport of holy joy, " It is good for us
to be with the cross; here let us make three
tabernacles, one in His feet, one in His hands,
and one in His side.   Here will I rest, here
will I watch; having always before my eyes
this divine book, to study in it the science of
salvation during the day, and as often as I awake
during the night."   He told them of the early
Christians, who, with St. Paul, gloried only in
the cross of Jesus, who painted it on their
doors, their walls, and their houses, and who
never performed the most trifling actions with·
out first making devoutly the sign of the cross,
which they considered both as a declaration of
their faith in the mystery of the Trinity, and
in the death and incarnation of Jesus Christ.
He concluded by reminding them that, if Jesus
Christ had loved them even unto the death of
the cross, they were bound to show their love

in return by a generous acceptance of the trials
of this life, which was the cross their heavenly
Father imposed upon them: and he assured
them that, if they carried the outward cross
bravely by the practice of religion, and the
inner cross meekly, by patience under suffering, they would not tremble, as the wicked
would do, with fear, but would rather be filled
like the Saints with joy and gladness, when,
at the last day, they should behold the sign
of the cross borne by angels as a banner of
light before the Son of man, coming in the
clouds with great power and majesty to judge
the world.

Many times during this little exhortation did
Marie press the crucifix which she wore round
her neck most devoutly to her bosom, promising faithfully to herself never, never to offend
the sweet Jesus any more; and she repeated
the same thing to her good friend the pilgrim
as they walked home after church. He smiled
as he answered:

"The ceremonies of Holy Week have then
had exactly the effect upon you which the
Church wishes them always to create in her

children. It is not merely to move us to pity and to love that she represents to us every circumstance of our Saviour's Passion,— from His entrance into Jerusalem, to the last seven words which He spoke upon the cross. She also wishes to convince us how great an evil is sin (since only the sufferings of a God could efface it), and to inspire us with a firm resolution of avoiding it for the future. Many an act of heroic virtue has been performed, inspired solely by this mournful commemoration of Passion-tide. The great of this world have made themselves poor and humble; kings have released their most treacherous subjects; men have pardoned their bitterest enemies, in honour of these days of sorrow and of love. One little instance of this I must give you; it is to be found in the history of St. John Gualbert. He had a brother named Hugo, who was slain by an enemy. In those wild days men too often avenged blood by blood; and John resolved to kill the murderer wherever he could find him. They met at last, and by God's providence it so happened it should be upon Good Friday; John instantly drew

bis swc;d, and would have slain his foe on the
spot, had not the other, who was unprepared
for combat, thrown himself at his feet, and besought him to spare his life for Christ's dear
sake, who had died for him and all sinners on
that day. John could not refuse to listen to
such a plea as this. To have spilt blood upon
Good Friday would have been sacrilege indeed;
so he not only pardoned the murderer of his
brother, he raised him from the ground, and
embraced him, remembering the kiss which
Jesus Christ would not refuse from the lips of
Judas. From that hour, we are told, his saintly
life began; and indeed it is easy to believe
that all the graces he afterwards received, and
by which he was made a saint in heaven at
last, were but the rewards of this one act of
charity, performed for the love of Jesus on the
very day on which Jesus had died for the love
of him."

Easter.[*]

All hail, Jesus!   Mary, all hail!

"OH, dear me," said Nina, as she and the
other children walked home after
"Tenebræ" on Good Friday evening,
"I shall be so glad when the church-bells
ring to-morrow; it is quite sorrowful not to
hear them once through the live-long day."

"That is just the reason why they are never
rung after the 'Gloria in excelsis' on Maunday
Thursday," said the pilgrim, with a smile.
"By this solemn stillness the Church wishes
to express her own grief, and to recall to our
minds the fear and sorrow of the Apostles at
the death of their divine Master, as also the
wonderful silence preserved by Jesus during
the time of His passion."

"But then they ought not to ring to-mor

* Continued from "Holy Week."

row," said Madeleine, "if they are a token of joy ; for our Blessed Saviour did not rise from the dead until the third day, which is Easter Sunday."

"Very true," he answered, "but there was formerly no Mass at all upon Holy Saturday and the one which is now said upon that day was celebrated at a very early hour upon Sunday morning. It is, therefore, properly speaking, the Mass of the Resurrection ; and, for this reason, it is said in white, the bells are rung, and the Church expresses her joy by the frequent alleluias with which the whole service is interspersed—alleluia being a Hebrew expression of gladness, signifying ' praise ye the Lord !' "

"Then had they no service at all upon Holy Saturday in those days !" asked Minette.

"They had the 'Tenebræ,' which we say on Good Friday afternoon, but which they only said after midnight on Saturday morning. Besides this, they were again assembled in the church at three o'clock in the evening, when the ceremonies of blessing the new fire, the paschal candle, and the baptismal font,

took place. These offices, with the baptism of
the catechumens, generally lasted until past
midnight, when the Mass of the Resurrection
was celebrated, as I have told you before."

"But what did they bless new fire for?"
said Nina, in a tone of wonder.

"The Church has always been in the habit
of invoking God's blessing on all things that
we use, but more especially upon those which
are afterwards to be dedicated to the service
of the Altar. She also regards this new fire
as an emblem of Jesus rising from the tomb;
and directly after it is blest, she uses it to light
the triple candles which represent the Blessed
Trinity, to signify to us that it is through
Christ alone we receive light to believe in this
wonderful mystery."

"If the triple candles represent the Blessed
Trinity, what, then, is the meaning of the
paschal candle? for I suppose it also must
mean something."

"Before it is lighted it is an image of Christ
in the sepulchre; the five grains of blest incense represent the spices with which His
sacred body was embalmed; and the five

boles, disposed in the form of a cross, in which they are placed, His five most precious wounds."

"1 was told once," said Minette, "that the paschal candle was blest by the deacon instead of the priest, to put us in mind of the sacred body of Jesus having been embalmed by the Disciples, and not by the Apostles; that the resurrection was not announced by these last, but by the holy women who declared it to them.'

"That is very probable," the pilgrim answered; "when the paschal candle is lighted it becomes a striking figure of Christ risen from the dead; and the rest of the lamps and candles in the church are lighted afterwards, to show us the resurrection of the faithful shall follow that of their divine Head."

"I suppose this is the reason it is taken out directly after Mass on Ascension-day, because then Christ went up into heaven, and was seen no longer upon earth."

"You are quite right, Madeleine; formerly the old paschal candle used to be broken into bits, and distributed among the faithful. And from thence we derive our present custom of

wearing Agnus Dei, which the Pope blesses
every seventh year of his reign."

"I have got a whole one Madame Margaret
gave me," said Madeleine; "it bears the image
of a lamb upon it."

"Yes," answered the pilgrim, "because it
represents Jesus Christ, the spotless Lamb of
God, who, as an old writer observes, 'should
be frequently brought to our memory by all
sorts of things.'"

"I do not very well know why those twelve
long lessons are read before the blessing of the
baptismal fonts," observed Madeleine.

"They were formerly read for the instruction of the catechumens, who were to be bap-
tised upon that night. They contain, as you
know, an account of the creation of the world,
of the deluge, the deliverance of the Jews out
of Egypt, besides many figures and prophecies
concerning the death and resurrection of our
Saviour. The tract said just before the blessing of the fonts, beginning, 'As the hart pants
for the fountains of water, so does my soul
pant after Thee, O God!' is, I think, beautifully expressive of the feelings of those who are

about to receive this sacrament of regeneration, and who should thirst, as it were, for the waters of baptism, by which they are to be made like innocent children in the sight of Almighty God."

"But we cannot thirst after baptism," said Nina, "because we have all received it when we were quite babies."

"Well, then," said the pilgrim, mildly, "let us try, at least, and thirst after the 'innocence of penance,' by which (if we have sinned) the purity of our baptismal robes is to be supplied."

"But why were people formerly always baptized upon Holy Saturday?" asked Marie.

"Because baptism is so true a figure of the resurrection," he replied; "for as Christ was laid in the sepulchre truly dead, and came out of it truly alive, so the soul, dead to God by original sin, comes forth from the baptismal waters reanimated with the new life of grace bestowed by the sacrament."

"I think the prayers said during the blessing of the fonts so very beautiful," said Minette.

"Yes," said the pilgrim; "and the ceremonies by which they are accompanied are

very expressive of the great dignity of the
sacrament for which these waters are consecrated. The priest divides the water in the
form of a cross, to teach us it confers grace by
means of Christ crucified. He touches it with
his hand, praying it may be free from all im-
pression of evil spirits. He makes the sign
of the cross thrice, to bless it in the name of
the Holy Trinity. He casts some of it towards
the four parts of the world, to show us the
grace of baptism flows all over the earth. He
blows thrice upon it in the form of a cross,
begging God to bless it by the infusion of His
Spirit, that it may receive the virtue of sanc-
tifying the soul. He plunges the paschal
candle thrice into it, praying the Holy Ghost
may descend into it, as He descended at the
baptism of Christ in the Jordan. He mixes
holy oil and chrism with it, to signify that
baptism consecrates us to God, and gives us
strength to fight with, and overcome our spiritual foes."

"Were not the neophytes formerly baptized directly after the blessing of the fonts?"
asked Minette.

" Yes," said the pilgrim ; " and the Litanies were then sung, as they still are, to obtain of God, through the intercession of His Saints, that the newly baptized might preserve the grace just conferred upon them. They also received holy Communion at Mass, with the rest of the faithful ; and it was sometimes the custom to give them afterwards a little milk and honey, which had first been offered at the Altar. This was intended to signify the state of spiritual infancy into which they had entered by being born again of the waters of baptism ; and also to show them that, by means of this sacrament, they had acquired a right to the kingdom of heaven, which is often mentioned in Scripture as a ' promised land, flowing with milk and honey.' "

" After Mass, however, to-morrow," said Minette, " I suppose we should return again to the contemplation of Jesus laid in the sepu chre."

" Yes," said the pilgrim ; " and the first fruit we should draw from such contemplation is, a firm resolution to die to sin, in order that we may rise to eternal life with Jesus." The

text is, to conceive a great desire of imitating
the pious zeal with which the disciples and
holy women sought to honour Him in His
burial."

"But how can we do that," asked Nina,
"since He has long since risen from the
dead?"

"Yet every time we go to holy Communion," returned the pilgrim, "we receive Him
not indeed dead, as He was in the sepulchre,
but living and glorious as He is now at the
right hand of the Father. Let us remember
that Joseph and Nicodemus wrapt His precious Body in clean linen, embalmed it with
spices, and laid it in a *new* sepulchre, where
no one had ever been buried before. Our
heart is as a living sepulchre, into which Jesus
Christ is graciously pleased to descend. It
should, therefore, be founded on a rock by our
firm resolution never more to commit sin, and
the entrance should be closed by our careful
avoidance of all its occasions. The white linen
cloths mark the purity by which it should be
adorned, and the spices are as the virtues with
which it must be embalmed, if we would give

Jesus a reception pleasing to Him , for it is
written : ' While the King was at his repose,
my spikenard sent forth the odour thereof.' "

" Madame Margaret used also to tell me,"
said Madeleine, " that the contemplation of
Jesus in the sepulchre should make the thought
of death less terrible to us. Because, before
His coming, it was only the punishment of
sin ; but now, being united to the merits of
his Passion and death, it has become the most
agreeable sacrifice we can make to our heavenly
Father."

" Master pilgrim," said Nina, " I wish you
would tell us something about the way in
which they keep Holy Saturday at Jerusalem."

" The ceremonies are exactly the same as
they are every where else in the Christian
world. But I think I never saw any thing
more magnificent than the appearance of the
church upon the night of Holy Saturday.
Ten thousand pilgrims were there, each holding a flambeau in their hands ; and the wide
galleries were filled with women and children,
every one carrying a lighted taper ; while
bishops, covered with gold and precious stones,

preceded by acolytes scattering incense, and
followed by numbers of white-stoled priests,
went in procession round the Holy Sepulchre,
singing hymns in honour of Him who on that
night had conquered death by rising from the
dead; and, in conclusion, men, and women,
and children, joined them in one joyful shout
of 'Alleluia, alleluia!' until it almost seemed
to me to be but the echo of that glorious
'alleluia' which St. John tells us is the song
of the ever-blessed saints in heaven."

When Marie returned home, she went as
usual to visit her pet lamb, which her grand-
father allowed her to keep in a paddock close
to the cottage. There she found Annette
(who had been sent by Pippo on a message
to the farmer) leaning over the gate, with her
eyes fixed on the little creature as it frisked in
the sunshine.

"What are you thinking of, St. Genevieve ?"
said Marie, smiling; "not about this lamb, I
dare say; but something very good about the
sweet and spotless Lamb of God, who suffered
this day on the Cross for us."

"No, indeed," said the poor shepherdess,

sadly, "my thoughts were not good at all,
Marie ; they were very bad, for I was envying
you this little lamb."

"Were you so very fond of it, then, when
you had the care of it ?" asked her wondering
companion.

"I loved all the creatures under my charge,
but I did not care for this one more than the
rest ; only I was just then thinking if it was
my own, I would sell it, and buy a covering
for my old grandmother, who is more crippled
than ever with rheumatism during these cold
easterly winds."

"But the Countess gave you ever so much
money the other day," said Marie, a little
doubtfully perhaps.

"Yes," said poor Annette, sobbing ; "and
Master Pippo took it from me, and swore he
would break all my bones if ever he was
found out. But where are you going, Marie ?"

"To tell the Countess, to be sure," said
Marie ; "she will certainly punish him for his
wickedness to you."

"You shall not tell her. I promised I would
not complain, and I won't ; and I did not in

tend to have told it to you; so you must promise you will not repeat what I have said,"
Annette sturdily replied.

With some difficulty, Marie gave the required promise; and then the little shepherdess
walked away to look after her flock, leaving
Marie with eyes fixed rather sorrowfully upon
her beloved lamb. She pondered over all the
great deeds of piety which the pilgrim had
told her were formerly practised in this week
of love. How kings had pardoned their enemies—how queens had washed the feet of the
poor—how rich men had spent thousands to
build hospitals for their reception. Her heart
had burned to copy their example, and now
she felt there was an occasion in which she
could do so.

"But they had so many other things,"
thought she, "and I have only one poor little
hurt." And she loved her lamb, and her
lamb loved her. It followed her wherever
she went, and was so full of fun and frolic
that she could have gladly spent hours in
watching its gambols. At last, however, she
called it to her; and, tying a string round its

neck, to prevent its being lost in going through the village, she set out for the Castle of Dris-bach ; but she had not gone half way, when she met the Countess returning from church.

" Well, Marie, how goes on the lamb ?" she asked, as soon as she perceived the little girl and her favourite.

" If you please, madame," said Marie, speak-ing in a very low voice, and with her eyes fixed on the ground, that her tears might not be visible to the lady, " I have come to ask your leave to give it to Annette."

" You mean the little shepherdess. Why, are you tired of it already ?"

" No, madame, I love it dearly ; but An-nette will sell it, and buy some clothing for her old grandmother with the money she gets for it."

" But why did not Annette buy some clo thing, then, with the money I gave her a short time ago ?"

Marie grew scarlet at this question.

" I know the reason, madame, but I cannot tell you, because I promised poor Annette that I would not do so."

" Will you sell the lamb to me, Marie ?"
said the Countess with a smile.

" Oh, yes," cried Marie; "I would much
rather give it back to you than have it sold to
some man who will certainly kill it." The
idea of her lamb killed, roasted, and eaten,
was too much for poor Marie's philosophy, and
she burst into tears.

"Then perhaps you would rather not sell
it ?"

" No, madame," said Marie ; " I have promised the sweet Jesus that I would do this
charity for His sake, and so I will." And she
led the lamb to the lady's feet, and returned
resolutely away.

" But you are going without your money ;
you are but a bad market-woman, I am afraid,"
said the Countess, who began to think Marie
might have been imposed upon by some pre-
tended tale of distress ; she therefore resolved
to give her some money now, and to inquire
as to the truth of Annette's story afterwards.
Marie came back, and held out one hand,
while she covered her face with the other to
conceal her tears. " Here," said the Countess,

"this is not the whole price of the lamb, but it is enough to clothe both Annette and her grandmother; and whenever you discover any poor but deserving objects, come to me, and I will pay you the rest of the money for them."

Marie hardly dared trust her voice to thank Madame Drisbach; and then, without casting a single glance at her bleating favourite, she set out for Annette's cottage; at first, it must be confessed, at a very slow pace, which, how-ever, grew brisker as she proceeded. The little shepherdess lived in a lonely hut on the brow of a hill, and Marie had no difficulty in discovering it, though she had never been there before. The miserable appearance of the old woman, as she lay in a corner of the room, half covered up by a tattered blanket, would have convinced Marie of the truth of Annette's story, if, indeed, it had ever come into the little girl's head to doubt it. At first she felt a good deal frightened, for she was not accustomed to speak freely to strangers; but, after some hesitation, she presented her little offering, and succeeded in making the old wo-man understand who she was, and why she had

brought it : the most difficult part of her visit
was now over, so by degrees she grew more at
her ease, and sat down and chatted with poor
Elise, who told her long stories of the cruelty
of Master Pippo, and of all that Annette had
to endure in order to earn a living for them
both. At last she took her leave, promising
(if her mother allowed it) often to return and
sit with her during the daily absence of her
granddaughter; and the bright smile of gratitude with which the poor woman received this
assurance more than repaid her for the loss of
her lamb. "Perhaps just at first," thought
Marie, as she walked towards the village, " it
is not quite so pleasant to talk to the old woman as it was to play with the lamb ; but then
I only pleased myself when I was with it, and
I am pleasing Jesus when I am talking to
Elise. That is the reason it is so much more
joyful afterwards : for I have played with the
lamb a hundred times, and never felt so happy
as I am feeling now." She was roused from
her reverie by Nina and Madeleine, who came
wild with delight to tell her that Madame
Drisbach had invited all the village-school

children to celebrate the Feast of the Resurrection by a grand dinner in the gardens of the castle.

The bells rung out merrily on Easter Sunday, and it was as bright and glorious a day as if it shared in the joy which all good Christians ought to feel at the resurrection of their divine Lord. The Countess waited herself on her young guests at table; and after their dinner was over, she gave them leave to wander whither they would through the spacious gardens, until the vesper-bell should summon them to church. The dinner-table was therefore soon deserted; and it was a pretty sight to see the young villagers, in their bright and many-coloured dresses, as they gradually separated into different groups, and wandered among the trees and flowers, or sat idly on the grass, filling the air with their gladsome voices. The children were perhaps the most cherished portion of Father Pierre's flock; and he felt as happy as the youngest among them while he watched them from the avenue, where he walked with Madame Drisbach. Suddenly he paused, and pointed to a group at the foot of an old walnut tree. Madeleine was busily engaged in plaiting wild flowers, and Marie half sat, half lay on the grass, watching her lamb, which had found her out, and was playing a thousand glad gambols at her feet; while Nina vainly tried to make it prisoner with the daisy chains handed to her by her sister as fast as she made them: the naughty lamb always managed to break away just as the flowery noose was fastened round its neck, leaving the broken wreath in the hands of its disappointed pursuer. Annette was the last of the party. Perhaps it was the only holyday she had enjoyed for the last two years of her life; but the Countess had insisted on Master Pippo's allowing her to come. So the poor shepherdess sat quietly by Marie, and once she kissed the little girl's hand, and the tears came into her eyes as she did so; for though she had a surly manner, she had a loving and affectionate heart.

"Well, my children, you have enjoyed yourselves to-day, I trust," said the Countess, as the joined them with Father Pierre.

"Oh, yes," cried the giddy Nina, "Easter is always such a joyful time; Easter, and the

young lambs, and the birds, and the flowers
all seem to come together, I think !"

" It is, and it ought to be a joyful time,"
said Father Pierre. " If we have sincerely
mourned with the disciples over the death of
Jesus, we may now as truly rejoice with them,
because ' the Lord has risen indeed.' "

" Good Friday was the most mournful of all
the days," said Marie simply. " In the evening the church felt *so* empty, because Jesus
was no longer there."

" It was the same feeling which made Magdalen weep, when she looked into the sepulchre
and saw Him not," observed the Countess,
smiling.

" How lovely is the history of her first meeting with Jesus," said Father Pierre; " her love
was so restless that she had not patience to wait
for the spices which the holy women were preparing in order to embalm the precious body
of their Lord, so she went on before them."

" As if to teach us diligence in all our religious duties," said the Countess : " for Scripture tells us she set out while it was yet dark."

" When she arrived at the sepulchre," Father

Pierre continued, "she found the stone removed, and she ran back to tell St. Peter and the
'other disciple whom Jesus loved' that 'they
had taken away the Lord, and she knew not
where they had laid him.' At this news the
disciples also came; and when they saw she
had spoken truly, they returned to their own
homes. 'But Mary stood at the sepulchre
weeping,' and, looking in, she saw two angels.
To many the vision would have given consola-
tion, but Mary could nowhere find comfort but
in Jesus. She was even so absorbed in grief,
that she forgot to ask the angels where He
was; though they, of all creatures, were most
likely to have been able to answer her question.
The tender heart of her divine Master could no
longer bear to see her so afflicted, and, turning back, she saw Him standing, ' but she knew
not that it was Jesus;' and when He asked
her why she wept, she only answered, 'If you
have taken *Him* away, tell me where you have
laid *Him*, and I will take *Him* away.' She
never named the object of her search. He was
so present to her own soul, it seemed to her
as if all the world must know that she loved

Jesus, sought Jesus, wept alone for Jesus, who alone was worthy of her tears. Jesus then took pity upon her, and called her by the dear familiar name of Mary. Joy nearly made her speechless, for she only said, 'Rabboni,' that is to say, Master, as she sank at His feet."

" How she must have loved Him at that instant!" said the Countess. " Doubtless her heart melted in tenderness as she anointed His feet at the Pharisee's supper, but then He had not died for her. She had not beheld Him on the Cross; she had not heard Him cry out in His agony, ' My God, My God! why hast Thou forsaken Me?' She had not known that the pardon He then gave her was to be written in His Blood."

" Neither had He spoken to her with such loving sweetness," observed Father Pierre. " Then He absolved her from her sins as one having power; now He speaks to her as an equal. ' I ascend to *My* Father and *your* Father, to *My* God and to *your* God.' The Father of Jesus! The Father of Magdalen!"

" And Magdalen was a sinner!" said little Marie, thoughtfully.

"Yes," said the Father; "but Jesus says Himself, that He came not to call the just, but sinners, to repentance. For them He lived—for them He died. And, as if to show the full extent of His loving mercy towards them, His first appearance recorded in the Gospel was to Magdalen, out of whom He had cast seven devils."

"But though this is the first appearance mentioned in the Gospel, Father Pierre, surely you believe that 'Mary, His Mother,' was really the first to behold her divine Son."

"Most devoutly do I believe it," answered Father Pierre. "She who sorrowed the most at His crucifixion was surely the first to behold Him in His glory. But who shall say what passed in that first meeting betwixt the human Mother and the Son Divine? No pen could describe it—no mind conceive it—no heart fathom its depth, or taste its sweetness. The inspired penmen are silent on the subject; and it is a mystery which only in eternity will be unfolded to our vision."

"It seems to me, also," observed the Countess, "as if the sweet Jesus suffered gelists to be silent on this subject, with a view to the encouragement and comfort of sinners. Among the holy women, His first appearance of which the Gospels speak was to Mary the sinner. Among the disciples, it was to St. Peter, who denied Him thrice, this favour was accorded."

"The pilgrim told us," said Madeleine, "that in the Church of the Holy Sepulchre at Jerusalem, there is a chapel called of 'the Apparition,' because tradition says it is the place where Jesus first appeared to His Blessed Mother."

"Perhaps it was so," said Father Pierre; "yet I like better to suppose, with the loving St. Bonaventure, that it was while she mourned like a dove in her desolate home, Mary first tasted this cup of ineffable bliss. Let us rejoice, my children, with the happiness of our beloved Mother on this glorious occasion; for this was, indeed, to her and to us all, the day of which the Prophet speaks, when he cries out, 'This is the day which the Lord hath made : let us be glad and rejoice therein.'"

"The Apostles also must have been full of

Joy, when they began to believe that Jesus really was risen from the dead," said Madeleine.

"To show their joy, and to honour this great event," answered Father Pierre, " they changed the observance of the Sabbath from the last day of the week to the first, the one upon which Jesus Christ arose. In the same spirit of gladness the early Church granted many privileges to her children during the Paschal time ; such as forbidding them to fast, and allowing them to stand up at prayer : these permissions were also extended to the Sundays throughout the year, because they are all consecrated to honour the mystery of the resurrection."

" That is the reason, then, that we all stand when the Angelus bell rings on Sunday," cried Nina, in great delight at this discovery.

" Exactly so. I suppose you also know the Paschal time lasts until the Feast of Pentecost, which occurs ten days after that of the Ascension."

" Ah," said Marie, " if the Apostles were rejoiced at the resurrection, they must have grieved at the ascension, when Jesus went up into heaven, so far away from them."

" I do not think so, my child; for they loved the divine pleasure of Jesus better than their own comfort."

"The pilgrim told me," said Madeleine, "that the print of our Blessed Saviour's foot is still to be seen in the rock from whence He ascended into heaven."

" I believe there is no doubt as to that fact," replied Madame Drisbach. " And it is said, that when the Empress St. Helen built a church upon Mount Olivet, they wished to cover this spot with a tablet of precious marble. But, though they fastened it carefully down with long golden nails, it was always removed by some invisible power, until at last they were obliged to leave it exposed to the veneration of the faithful."

" The Mount of Olives was the place where Jesus suffered His agony, was it not?" asked Marie.

" Yes," said Father Pierre; " and it was just that the disciples should behold Him glorified on the very spot where some of them had seen

Him humbled to the dust by the anticipation
of His coming Passion. Forty-three days after
this sorrowful evening, therefore, He led them
thither once more; and, lifting up His hands,
He blessed them, and then ascended into heaven
by His own strength and power; for He need-
ed no car of fire, as Elias did of old, to bear
Him from the earth."

"And He was attended," added Madame
Drisbach, "by all the Saints of the old law,
singing, with the Prophet-king, 'Lift up your
gates, O ye princes! and be ye lifted up, O
eternal gates! and the King of Glory shall enter
in;' while crowds of angels, descending to welcome their Sovereign, filled all heaven with
their harmony, as they joined in the triumph-
ant response, 'Who is the King of Glory?
The Lord of Power; He is the King of Glory.'"

"But the disciples did not see all this?"
said Madeleine, doubtfully.

"No," said Father Pierre; "but we learn
from St. Paul that the saints of the old law
did accompany Jesus on this occasion; and the
angels assured the disciples He had ascended
into heaven, as He would descend on the last

day, when, He tells us Himself, He shall be
accompanied by a multitude of holy spirits.
We may believe, therefore, that He was so at
tended on the Feast of the Ascension."

"Can you tell us about the processions on
the Rogation-days?" said Madeleine.

"Yes," said Father Pierre, "they were established by St. Mammertus, Bishop of Vienne,
to avert the many calamities which afflicted his
country. Frightful earthquakes had occurred,
which overturned the most massive buildings;
wild beasts are said to have left the woods and
rushed through the streets; and a fearful fire
took place while the people were assembled in
the church upon Easter night. As soon as this
last misfortune was made known, every one fled,
to save, if possible, his own habitation, and the
Saint remained alone at the Altar, endeavour-
ing to appease the divine anger with tears and
supplications. It was then that he formed the
idea of the rogations—which word simply
means any form of prayer or supplication—
and no sooner had he done so, than the fire
ceased, and the people all returned to the church
to give thanks to Almighty God. The Sain'

then acquainted them with the promise he had made to God of offering up public prayers for the safety of the country. They entered into his design with joy, and, on each of the three days before the Feast of the Ascension, they sung the Litanies in a public procession with great piety and devotion. This pious custom spread rapidly through France, and from thence, I believe, it soon was established in most countries of Europe."

"Would you like to hear a story of the Rogation-days, which a countryman of mine once told me, and he assured me it happened exactly as he related it?"

"Oh, yes; pray tell it to us, madame," cried all the children together, with one voice.

"But first," said the Countess, "I must tell you that I intend to invite all the village children to dinner on the Feast of Pentecost, and whichever has the best character among her companions shall be queen of the day, and shall be allowed to ask me any favour she pleases; and, if Father Pierre judges it to be reasonable, I promise beforehand to grant it."

"Oh, thank you, madame," cried all the

children; "and I know who will be queen, if
I can help it," said Madeleine, in a low voice,
as she looked at Marie.

"And I know who will be queen, if I can
help it," thought Marie; "for she is better than
any of us;" and her eyes fell on the little
shepherdess, sitting silently at her side.

"And now for the story, madame," cried
Nina. "Pray, what is it called?"

"If you like," said the Countess, smiling, we
will call it 'Mimi's grave, or Rogation-day.'"

"Well," said Father Pierre, "I trust, madame, you will have finished your story before
the bells announce vespers; for it is right that
in the church, where they begin, we should
finish our rejoicings over the happy festival of
Easter."

HYMN FOR EASTER-SUNDAY.

O filii et filiæ.

YE sons and daughters of the Lord!
The King of glory, King adored,
This day Himself from death restored

All in the early morning gray
Went holy women on their way,
To see the tomb where Jesus lay.

Of spices pure a precious store
In their pure hands those women bore,
To anoint the sacred Body o'er.

Then straightway one in white they see
Who saith, " Ye seek the Lord; but He
Is risen, and gone to Galilee."

This told they Peter, told they John;
Who forthwith to the tomb are gone,
But Peter is by John outrun.

That self-same night, while out of fear
The doors were shut, their Lord most dear
To his Apostles did appear.

But Thomas, when of this he heard,
Was doubtful of his brethren's word,
Wherefore again there comes the Lord.

" Thomas, behold my side," saith He ;
" My hands, my feet, my body see,
And doubt not, but believe in Me."

When Thomas saw that wounded side,
The truth no longer he denied ;
" Thou art my Lord and God !" he cried

Oh, blest are they who have not seen
Their Lord, and yet believe in Him !
Eternal life awaiteth them.

Now let us praise the Lord most high,
And strive his name to magnify
On this great day, through earth and sky

Whose mercy ever runneth o'er ;
Whom men and Angel Hosts adore
To Him be glory evermore.

MIMI'S GRAVE;

OR,

Rogation-Day.[*]

THE hawthorn was just bursting into bloom, and lilacs and laburnums were beginning to be bowed down by their weight of blossom, when a weary-looking traveller rode up to the door of a cottage in Bretagne, and inquired the distance to the nearest town. The answer was not favourable. The way was long, and the roads were bad; and the traveller looked ruefully from the tired horse he rode to a group of merry children, who were laughing and chatting, as they took their supper beneath the shadow of an old hawthorn tree. The good woman of the cottage, observing his looks of vexation, said, with some hesitation, that if the gentleman chose to alight, her husband would look to his horse, and he himself

[*] Continued from the "Festival of Easter."

was welcome to join their family supper; and
afterwards he could either proceed on his journey, or remain at the cottage during the night.
The traveller paused for a moment; but the
cottage, the woman, and the children, all looked cleaner than cottages, women, and children
generally look in Brittany. So, giving his horse
to the care of the peasant, who had just come
in from the fields, he sat down beneath the
hawthorn, to share the supper of the children.
As he understood the dialect of the country,
he was soon perfectly at home among them;
and they were all in high glee when the peasant joined them, with the assurance that the
horse was rubbed down, and settled for the
night. The traveller thanked him, and added,
" This is fine weather for the country, my friend."
But the peasant shook his head, and answered
" Fine weather for you gentlemen that rid
about for your amusement, but not fine weather
for the country. Six weeks without a drop of
rain; the land is dried up and parched, as if
it had been baked in an oven."

" There will be rain in three days—fine, soft
rain—and it will fall lightly on Mimi's grave,"

said a childish voice close to the traveller. He
turned in extreme surprise, and beheld a little
girl, whom he had noticed before, but whom
he had fancied to be almost an infant, from the
fact of her being laid in a kind of cradle.

"And how do you know there will be rain
in three days, my child?" he asked, after gaz-
ing a moment on her soft blue eyes and delicate face.

"Do you not know," she answered, in her
sweet, plaintive voice, and without any of the
bashfulness of childhood, "that the Feast of the
Rogation begins to-morrow, and the priest and
the people, old men and young men, women
and children, will go forth over the open country, calling on the Saints of God to help them.
And the Saints will pray to God, and He will
hear the voice of His beloved ones; He will
bless the fields, He will bless the fountains, He
will bid soft rain drop down from heaven, to
gladden the peasant's heart, and to sweeten the
peasant's toil. It will fall softly everywhere,
but softest of all upon Mimi's grave."

"What a strange child!" said the traveller
"Who is this Mimi of whom she speaks?"

"It is herself, sir," said the poor mother; "she always speaks like that, for she is wonderfully wise, though not quite so young as you would think her; she has been a cripple from her birth, which will be eight years this summer."

"And does she think she is dying, that she speaks so about her grave?"

"She *is* dying, sir," said the poor woman, suppressing a sob. "They tell me that in a few days it will all be over. It is a hard thing to lose a child," she added, struggling to speak calmly; "one, too, whose helplessness calls for double love and double care; and who is so full of holy thoughts and words, that it is like listening to one of God's little angels only to hear her."

"Mimi often sees God's little angels in her dreams," said the child, whose quick ear had caught her mother's last words; and soon she will see them face to face, while the rain is falling so gently on her grave."

"Do not say so my child," said the poor woman; "I will bring the portion of the poor to the cross, where a station will be made to morrow; and they will pray for my sick little one when they find it there."

"Their prayers will be heard in heaven, mother."

"They will, they will," said the woman eagerly; "I will carry you to the foot of the cross to-morrow; and when Father Joseph prays before it, his blessing will fall upon you, my child, as well as on the flowers of the field."

"When Father Joseph's blessing falls on her soul, Mimi will pass away to her God," said the child, in the same strange and meditative tone of voice.

"No, no," answered the mother; "my child will grow strong and well beneath the blessing of God's holy servant. And when the sweet rain of summer falls, Mimi will be blithe and happy as the birds and flowers."

"The birds and flowers are in their own home on earth; but heaven is the home of all sick children (Father Joseph told me so), and there only shall Mimi grow well and happy."

The poor mother made no answer; she only stooped to kiss the child; and when Mimi felt that she was weeping she put her arms round the woman's neck, wiped the hot tears from her eyes, and tried to console her with an air of affectionate earnestness, which gave her for an instant, the appearance of being the elder of the two. Two or three of the boys interrupted this little scene by asking Mimi if she would come with them to the great cross, as they were going to dress it for the station that was to be held there during the procession. She smiled ; and the mother cautioning them to be careful of her, they lifted up the cradle in which she lay, and, followed by the rest of the laughing children, they set off joyously together.

" Where are they going to, and what are they going to do ? " asked the traveller, who was puzzled by the sudden disappearance of the merry group.

" Mimi told you, sir. To-morrow we go in procession, and sing the litanies to obtain God's blessing on the fruits and grain of the earth ; and there is an old cross near here which the children always dress with flowers and garlands, as it is one of the stations where the people stop to pray on their way. I am going my self, sir, to leave 'the portion of the poor' at the foot of the cross; perhaps you would like to come with me, as you seem curious about it?"

"I should like very much to join my merry little friends there," said the stranger; "but what do you mean by 'the portion of the poor?'"

"Why, sir, we have a custom in this country, that whenever any one is sick among us, we put aside a portion of food from the family meals, and lay it at the foot of the nearest cross on the roadside. When poor people pass that way, they know it has been left there for their use; and, in gratitude, they kneel down, and say a prayer for the sick persons, that they may either recover, or die a happy death, as God, in His wisdom, shall please to direct. Here is Mimi's portion," she added, uncovering a porringer. "For three months I have made this offering every day; but it is all in vain, for the child is dying as fast as she can."

"Not in vain," said the traveller, gently; "M.mi will go to heaven if she die now; perhaps were she spared she might live a discontented cripple."

"I often think of that sir; and try to com

fort myself by the thought of her eternal happiness ; and she longs so much to go to heaven, that I do not believe she could be happy as long as she remained in this world. And now here we are at the holy cross, which I have brought you to visit."

The traveller took off his hat, and knelt for a moment ; but he soon rose again, for the children were too merry and boisterous to admit of a longer prayer. One little urchin had climbed on his brother's shoulder, and was twining a long wreath of ivy round the arms of the cross ; two or three others were half hidden in the heavy branches of hawthorn which they stuck into the ground at its foot, and which they had adorned with knots and streamers of gay-coloured ribands ; and the little girls were all on their knees, making carpet work around it of primrose, moss, cowslips, and daisies. Mimi lay in her cradle, watching their proceeding with an air of quiet pleasure ; and the other children often came to show her some new treasure brought from the woods and fields, or to kiss her little shrivelled hands ; for they all doated on the gentle child, and sought as much

as possible to make her a sharer in their pleas-
ures. "Do not move the little crosses," said
she earnestly; "the next cross placed here will
be for Mimi." She alluded to the little crosses
which the peasants of Brittany always placed
at the foot of any great cross where a funeral
has paused on its way to the church. "You
will put my cross there, will you not?" she
continued, speaking to one of the elder boys;
"just between that great bunch of cowslips
and primroses."

"No, Mimi," said the boy affectionately;
"I will place no little cross for you there.
But I will lay you there yourself to-morrow;
and when the blessing falls upon you, you
will feel quite well and strong again; and
from this high ground you will be able to see
the procession all over the country."

"I shall see the procession until it reaches
this cross," persisted Mimi; "but after that I
shall see it no more."

"But you must see it, Mimi; and you must
look out for me; for I am to be one of the
choir-boys, and I shall walk all over the country in my new white alb and beautiful red sash.

I am so glad I am a choir-boy now; last year
Father Joseph thought me too young; but I
am ever so much older and taller than I was
last year, you know, Mimi," said the boy, drawing himself proudly up.

"But you must be very wise, Pierre; and
you must not think too much about your alb
and red sash, though I know they are very
pretty to look at, and nice to wear," said Mimi
gently.

"And pray what must I think of, Mimi?
You are so wise, that perhaps you can tell me."

"Father Joseph told me we must think of
the Saints who are at that moment, perhaps,
praying to God to help us. We must think
how happy they are now, and how they owe
all their happiness to the good Jesus, who
came from heaven to teach them how they
should walk through the world, meekly, humbly, gently, as He did, not caring for the
praises or riches of men, but only seeking the
will and pleasure of their heavenly Father."

"Why, Mimi, you would preach nearly as
good a sermon as Father Joseph himself," said
the traveller, with a smile.

"It was Father Joseph told it all to me, sir," said Mimi. "He often sits by me, and tells me things about God and His holy angels, that make my heart quite full of joy and longing to behold them."

She was interrupted by Father Joseph himself, who, having heard from one of the children of the arrival of a stranger in the village, had come to offer him a room at his house, knowing well the discomforts he would meet with in a Breton cottage. But the traveller had become so much interested in the little cripple, that he was at first rather unwilling to accept this kind offer. At last, however, it was settled that he should pass the night at the curé's, and the next morning join Mimi and her mother at the station of the cross, where they were to await the coming of the grand procession. As he walked back to the village with the priest, he expressed his wonder at the extraordinary devotion of so young a child as Mimi.

"She is really a little angel," answered Father Joseph. "But I have often observed t thus with young children whose bodies are bowed down by disease. Their good heavenly

Father is never unmindful of His little ones,
He gives to the spirit the strength and joy
which, for His own wise purposes, He has
denied to their suffering limbs."

"But do you really think she will die to-
morrow, as she says she will?" asked the traveller doubtfully.

"Why not?" answered the old man. "God
sometimes gives this knowledge to His chosen
ones; and who can be more dear to Him than
an innocent, suffering, and patient child—since
it has been said, 'Of such as these is the Kingdom of Heaven.' But this poor Mimi's death
is already written on her face; and I doubt
not she will celebrate the Feast of the Ascension with the angels in heaven."

When the traveller returned to the cottage
next morning, he found four of the children,
who were to act as choir-boys, starting off in
high glee for the church; they told him Mimi
and her mother were already established at the
station of the cross; and thither he instantly
directed his footsteps. He found Mimi lying
in her cradle, and sheltered from the rising sun
by large boughs of hawthorn, which her bro-

thers had hung over her head. Her little hands were joined in prayer; and, with her blue eyes raised to heaven, she looked so fair, so delicate an l fragile, that he no longer found it difficult to believe she would die as soon as the blessing of the priest had passed over her soul. " How is it with you to-day, Mimi?" he asked; and she answered, with an unearthly smile, " Better, thank you, sir. The little angels were with me all night long, and they said they would come to-day to take me back to heaven with them."

" Hush, Mimi," said the poor woman. " The Angelus bell is ringing, and the procession will soon leave the church now. If you stand here, sir, you will see it as it comes up the village and across the fields. And it is my husband who carries the holy banner, and one of my boys is the cross-bearer. Father Joseph chose them for their good conduct," she added, with a look of proud delight.

" Ah," sighed Mimi very gently, " I hope poor little Pierre will not think too much of his white alb and beautiful sash."

" You must not blame him too much for that, Mimi," said the smiling traveller; " it is very natural he should think a little about it just at first. But I dare say he will be very devout and attentive for all that."

"Oh, yes," said the woman; "when once the procession sets out, I am sure he will; for he is a very good boy, though sometimes a little giddy.—Now, sir, the procession is leaving the church, and you can see it quite well here."

It was a pretty sight to see, as the traveller looked at it from the high hill on which the cross of the station stood. The silver cross of the parish glittering in the morning sun, and the old velvet banner, with the image of the patron Saint of the village embroidered on it, floating heavily on the morning air. Cross and banner were followed by a long train of peasants, men in their fawn-coloured dresses, and women with the snow-white cap of the country; and as the procession left the village, he could trace it, now spreading into the open fields, now winding along the brow of the hill, now descending deep into the valleys. Suddenly it seemed to pause. "What are they stopping for?" he asked the woman. "They are making

a station, sir, at the chapel of our patron Saint;
you cannot see it, for those trees stand just
before it." " Now they are moving on again,"
said the traveller ;—" but stay ; they have once
more halted." " Father Joseph is blessing the
fountain which supplies the village with water
He asks the blessing of God upon all things
here below, the grain, the plants, the trees, and
the waters of the earth," said the woman—
" Now, sir, they have made yet another pause.
It is at a little hermitage at the foot of this
hill; they will be here almost directly ; see,
the cross is just beginning to ascend, and, hark,
you can already catch the voices of the chanters." She knelt down while she spoke, for
the prayer of the people as they ascended the
hill came distinctly to their ears. The chanters
named all the Saints in the litany ; and at each
name old men and young men, women and
children, responded by an *Ora pro nobis*, that
floated over hill and valley, filling all the airs
of heaven with its tones of devotional sweetness.

" They are coming—they are coming," said
Mimi faintly ; " raise me up, mother, that Father
Joseph may bless me as he goes along."

"Lie still, my child; lie still," said the mother; "you cannot see them yet—*Ora pro nobis—Ora pro nobis*," she repeated, as the prayer rose louder and louder in the morning air.

"They are coming—they are coming," persisted Mimi. "I see the angels of the people, who walk before them, and offer up their prayers to God."

"Hush—hush, my child; you rave," said the mother; "angels are invisible, though, I doubt not, they are indeed this day among the people."

"And the Saints," murmured Mimi, regardless of her mother's words—"Lo! here they come! Oh, what a crowd of happy spirits. The saint of a hundred years and the infant of a few days old. The sinner who has washed out his guilt in floods of tears, and the innocent child who has brought the robes of its baptism unsullied to the judgment seat of God. I see them all—I see them all! Oh, bright and happy children of God—*Ora pro nobis—Ora pro nobis!*"

"Alas, she raves, she raves!" cried the

mother, wringing her hands—"she will die
before they have reached the spot, and before
she has received the blessing that is to make
her well."

"Not yet, not yet," said Mimi; "hold me
up yet a moment longer, mother, for now they
come indeed, the children, the people, and the
priest. I shall not die until I have received
his blessing."

It was even as Mimi said. The procession
had reached the brow of the hill, and was
wending slowly towards them.

First came the good man of the cottage in his
peasant dress, carrying the consecrated banner.
Then one of his sons in white alb over a red
soutaine, holding so that all could see it the
cross of the parish; on each side of him children bearing flambeaux; then the choristers,
after them the children of the Christian school,
and the Sisters of Charity with the young girls
whom they had undertaken to educate, and
they were followed by the old priest and his
two assistants in white surplices and gilded
stoles.

An uncounted multitude of people walked

after him,—for every house in the parish sent
two or more of its inhabitants to assist at the
pious ceremony, and to invoke the blessing of
Heaven on the produce of the country. Those
whom age or sickness prevented from attend-
ing, told their beads as they lay on their
humble beds, or knelt in prayer before the
doors of their cottages, while the procession
passed before them. The priest had now
reached the station of the cross, and knelt
down, surrounded by the acolytes and other
assistants; his head was bowed in prayer, so
that he did not perceive Mimi in her cradle at
a very little distance from him. The child
watched him for a moment anxiously, and
then she said :

"The Angels are going—the Saints are
going. Mother, tell him to bless me quickly
—for Mimi is going too."

"Stay, dear child, stay ; in a few moments
he will come and bless you."

"Tell him to make haste, mother, for Mimi
is going quickly."

The bewildered mother half raised the child
from the cradle, dreading she knew not what,

and she could hear her still murmuring on
her bosom: "Tell him to make haste! Tell
him to make haste!" "I cannot leave her,
I dare not leave her in this state," the poor
creature half cried aloud. The traveller saw
her embarrassment, and he was just stepping
forward to apprise Father Joseph of the situa-
tion of the child, when Pierre, who, from his
station among the children, had been watching Mimi in complete forgetfulness of his alb
and sash, sprang forward, and touching the
priest, said hurriedly:

"My father, Mimi wants your blessing; she
is dying."

Thus aroused, Father Joseph rose from his
knees, and advanced towards Mimi. The
dying child stretched out her arms when she
saw him coming, and bowed down her little
head; he laid both his hands in fervent blessing on it; and even before he removed them,
the soul of Mimi had departed to the society
of the angels about whom she so loved to
dream. This unexpected event caused some
delay and confusion in the order of the procession; at last, however, the traveller under-

took to carry the consecrated banner; and the
peasant who had hitherto borne it was thus
enabled to remain with his weeping wife by
the side of their dear little angel they had lost.
Father Joseph felt very grateful to the stranger
for his kindness on this occasion; and after
the ceremonies of the day were over, he invited
him to prolong his stay at his house for a few
days longer: an offer most gladly accepted;
for the traveller wished to join in the devotions
of the Rogation-days which yet remained to
be celebrated, and was anxious, besides, to
attend the funeral of poor Mimi, in whose fate
he had become so deeply interested.

The little child was buried the next day;
and at his own request he was one of those
who carried the coffin, and assisted in lower-
ing it into the grave. The earth they heaped
upon it was dry and hard; and as he recalled
Mimi's words, " That rain would soon fall
upon her grave," he could not help feeling
certain her strong faith would be justified, and
that the good God would not refuse His blessing to the fervent supplications which had been
offered up to Him that day.

He carried the consecrated banner before
the priest on the last of the three Rogation-
days; and when they paused in the church-
yard to pray for the souls of the faithful departed, he went a little aside and knelt down
on Mimi's grave close by her weeping mother.
Yet he did not go there to pray for the innocent child, but rather to ask her prayers; for
he, as well as all those who had known her,
and had seen her die, firmly believed her to
be at that moment a happy little angel in
the presence of her God.   That same evening
he bade adieu to Father Joseph, for he intended
to depart at dawn the next day, and to hear the
mass of the Ascension in an adjoining parish.
Pierre was to bring him his horse from the
cottage, and to awaken him by throwing a
pebble at his window.   As soon as he heard
the signal, he arose, dressed himself, and
opened the house-door.

"I have brought you your horse, sir," said
Pierre, as soon as he saw him; and he added
in a lower tone, "the rain has been falling softly
—*so softly*—all night long upon Mimi's grave."

It was very true; the air was sweet with the

smell of the up-turned earth and fresh-fallen rain. The flowers had revived, the fields were green, the birds were singing merrily on the trees, and every creature and every thing seemed rejoicing in the May showers which had visited them during the night, as an especial gift from God's own hand.

The traveller rode thoughtfully away. And when, in another country and in other days, he heard people complaining of the scantiness of the crops and the badness of the weather, he used to tell them of the faith of the simple peasants of Brittany, which taught them ever to speak to God of their temporal as well as their spiritual necessities, remembering the gracious promise of their Saviour: "Ask and receive, that your joy may be made full."

As the Countess concluded her story, the castle bell tolled, that the children might assemble before vespers; and they now came from the gardens, and being formed into orderly procession, walked quietly to the church.

"How fond they are of religious conversation," said the Countess to Father Pierre; "if spoke half as seriously to children in England as I do to these little ones, they would be tempted to tell me I was too fond of *preaching*."

"The Tyrolese are a singularly religious people," replied Father Pierre. "They love religion, and to read or speak about it; and in the church there will hardly be a wandering glance or an absent mind among the little troop who were but now running like wild sheep about your gardens, or listening, with all their eyes and ears, to your story of ' Rogation Day.'"

Our Lady the Deliverer.

The severe winter which ushered in the eighteenth century, advanced with such rude and tempestuous strides, that it seemed to prefigure to the minds of men the miseries, convulsions, and ruin, which that century of troubles carried in its womb. Calamities of divers kinds afflicted the earth; and the sea, swept by tempests, covered the shores with the sad wrecks of its fury.

But, in spite of unruly waves and boisterous winds, commerce, ever venturesome in pursuit of wealth, was sending her ships over the seas of the world. A merchant ship from Havre fatigued by its long course, heavily laden, and carrying many guns, was returning from Lisbon, on the 12th of February, 1700, through a most tempestuous sea, running many risks, but reckoning on her good equipment to reach the port in safety.

A Norman sailor, who was on board, could not avert his eyes from a point on the horizon, where he kept his sight fixed on a speck, which kept increasing as the ship neared.

" If our Lady the Deliverer comes not to our aid," said he at length, to a passenger, " we shall pass a terrible night."

" What title is this you give to our Lady ?" asked the passenger.

" You must certainly be a Portuguese, or a native of some outlandish place, not to have heard of this celebrated pilgrimage," replied the sailor : " it takes its origin, they say, from the time of the first apostles of the country. For more than six hundred years, a miraculous image of our Lady had been venerated in the country between Caen and Bayeux, when the rude men of the north came and ravaged France. Although we are certainly descended from these Normans, I hope we bear no resemblance to them in impiety. . The Church, at least as it formerly did, does not now pray to be delivered from us. Our Lady's chapel was destroyed by these barbarians, and its sacred image buried beneath its ruins. The pilgrimage became a sad spot for those who remembered it, and who had often there invoked the assistance of our Lady the Deliverer, whose powerful aid was sought by distressed mariners at sea. Two centuries passed away * * * *

"The remains of the chapel had been used in the erection of cottages, and the land had been cultivated, so that the precise spot on which it had stood was forgotten. Nobody had ever been able to discover the holy image. But now our dear Lady took compassion on the people who had become Christians. It was during the reign of Henry I. of France, when our Duke William set out for the conquest of England. Thus has the circumstance been told me,—

"But see," said the narrator, interrupting his discourse, "how the darkness increases. The sky seems covered with a black mantle. It is not yet mid-day, and we can scarce see before us."

"And this February rain is most bitterly cold," said the passenger : "it seems to me that our ship has got into a bad sea. We are running, as you will soon see, across the reefs of the isle of Ouessant."

The sailor made the sign of the cross. The passenger did the same, with a sigh.

"May our Lady the Deliverer be our pilot !" continued the Norman : "we shall stand in great need of her assistance" * * *

"Well, I was telling you how she took compassion on the poor people, and wished to restore her pilgrimage. The shepherd of a neighbouring lord discovered a very singular occurrence. Every day he saw one of his sheep leave the flock, and wander abroad without any molestation on the part of the dogs. He found that the animal went into a small meadow where the grass was finer and fresher than anywhere else; but, to his suprise, he saw that instead of browsing there, he turned up the earth with his feet. For several days this sheep took no nourishment,—which, however, did not prevent its being one of the fattest of the flock. When tired with its labour, the sheep lay down on the spot until evening, when it returned to the fold at the shepherd's call. These facts were mentioned to Baudoin, the lord of the manor, who was much astonished, and came to the spot, accompanied by his friends, to ascertain the truth of the story. He then ordered his labourers to dig up the soil on the spot where the sheep had barely scratched to the depth of a foot; when, to the delight of all assembled, after an hour's labour, they discovered the venerable image of our Lady the Deliverer. It was transported, amid the rejoicings of all the neighbouring people, to the great Church at Bayeux. But what followed will doubtless appear more strange to you; for the next morning the statue had disappeared; and on seeking for it, it was found in the precise spot where it had been discov

ered on the preceding day. This circumstance
seemed to show that the ancient chapel had
stood on this ground, and that it was our Lady's
desire that it should be rebuilt in the same
place. This was accordingly done. Henceforth the pilgrimage was revived, and has continued uninterrupted to the present day. During
which time, our Lady the Deliverer has worked
many astonishing cures and wonders."

At this moment, an order from the captain
interrupted the narrative. The sailor was
called to his work. The passengers themselves laboured at the pumps, for the ship
was filling from several parts. Premature
night brought an increase of the terrors with
which a tempest at Cape Finisterre is ever attended. We might draw upon our imagination for a description of the storm, but we
prefer not to interrupt the simple narrative of
the legend by our own words.

The sailors had said their night prayers, and
were chanting the "*Ave Maris Stella*" in their
rough, but plaintive melody. The winds and
the waves replied in sounds of fury. A long,
and terrible night ensued ; no sun appeared

on the next morning; but some faint gleams
of light, which they were glad to call day,
burst upon the shattered vessel; for, carried
along by the raging waters, the ship had lost
all her rigging and sails; her cannon, rudder,
and compass, were gone. Hurried along by
the winds, she was about to capsize, when the
Norman sailor cried out,—

"We are all lost, unless we implore the all-
powerful aid of our Lady the Deliverer!"

All the sailors instantly uncovered their heads
and kneeling, as well as they could, made a vow
to make a pilgrimage to her sanctuary.

"If the holy Virgin can hear us," said Charles
Ferret, falling on his knees, "I also heartily
invoke her aid." His younger brother imitated
his example. Instantly there came a calm;
the winds subsided; every heart beat with
emotion, while the shattered vessel gained its
position, and floated safely on the tranquil sea.

"O, Lady, our Deliverer! I am yours for
ever," cried the youngest brother.

The second brother, however, still remained
unmoved. His elder reproaching him, he
replied:

"I see in what has happened the goodness of our God, who comes to our assistance; but I am not prepared to abjure my religion."

"Behold with your own eyes my unhappy brother," cried out the captain; and he pointed to the top of the first mast, left uninjured, around which a soft light was seen to play, and in it the figure of a heavenly Virgin was distinctly seen. She held in her hands an infant, whose outstretched hands extending over the ocean, seemed to call upon it to be calm. The second brother, touched by this marvel, could doubt no longer, but declared his belief in the intercession of Mary. Meanwhile the ship, though deprived of her principal powers of motion, calmly floated into the port of Havre.

The first act of the brothers on their landing was to proceeed to the nearest church, and there abjure their errors. They afterwards placed themselves at the head of the pilgrimage of the ship's crew and passengers to the chapel of our Lady the Deliverer, to thank her for her miraculous intervention, and to have masses of thanksgiving offer d at her shrine

Pentecost *

All hail, Jesus! Mary, all Hail!

PENTECOST is come at last! and I am so glad," cried Nina, as she joined the other children, who were sitting with the pilgrim under the shade of a weeping-willow which grew before Marie's door.

" Yes," answered Marie; " but we are not to go to Madame Drisbach's until after vespers; because then we shall have a long evening in her beautiful gardens."

" And every one in the village will be there. She says all the villagers, both old and young, must celebrate the Feast of Pentecost with her," added Nina, joyfully; " and won't you also come, master pilgrim, and tell us some nice long story under the trees?"

" Yes," the pilgrim replied, with a very sad

' Continued from the " Festival of Easter."

smile, " I will come and tell you my own story
if you wish to hear it."

" Indeed I do wish to hear it," said Nina
" and so does every one else too. People are
always wondering why you came here, and
what sort of business you can possibly have
with the Countess of Drisbach."

" Very stupid in them to be so curious,"
said Madeleine, not very well pleased at Nina's
rudeness. " Now, master pilgrim, do pray go
on reading to us, as you did before Nina interrupted us."

The pilgrim took up his book, and went on
reading the account of the descent of the Holy
Ghost, from the Acts of the Apostles.

" But then," said Madeleine, as soon as he
had finished, " the Jews must have had a Pentecost as well as the Christians, for it says, ' when
the days of Pentecost were accomplished ?' "

" Pentecost was one of the three great festi
vals of the Jews," said the pilgrim ; " it was
called the ' feast of the first fruits,' because, on
this day they offered to God two loaves of bread
made from the wheat-harvest of the year, be
fore which it was not lawful to eat bread of

that crop. Every person also was obliged to give his first-fruits of wheat, barley, apricots, grapes, figs, olives, and dates. They brought them to the temple in bands, attended by one or more musicians, playing on the flute, and preceded by an ox destined for sacrifice, with gilded horns, and a crown of olives upon its head."

"Father Pierre told me," observed Madeleine, " that the Christian Pentecost was also a festival of first-fruits, since upon it St. Peter converted three thousand persons, who might properly be considered as the first-fruits, of the religion Christ came to establish upon earth."

"I knew a Jew once," said Minette, "and he used to call the Jewish Pentecost the feast of the law."

" It was so called," answered the pilgrim, " because it was also considered as a day of thanksgiving for the old law given on Mount Sinai. God having willed the new law to begin, by the descent of the Holy Ghost, on the same day on which the old law had formerly commenced, and on which it was now to be abolished for ever."

"But the Apostles were not frightened by the coming of the Holy Ghost, as the Israelites were by the presence of God on Mount Sinai," observed Minette.

"No," said the pilgrim; "and yet the Holy Ghost descended in person on the apostles, while God only spoke to the Jews by the voice of an angel. But the old law was a law of fear, given in thunder and lightning, and engraved upon tables of stone; while the new law was a law of love, filling men with grace and sweetness, and written in their hearts by the finger of the Holy Ghost, who is Himself the author and infinite source of love."

"Were the Apostles in the temple when the Holy Ghost descended on them?" asked Marie.

"They are supposed to have been assembled in the house of Mary, the mother of John Mark, one of the disciples of Jesus; and were engaged in prayer with the Blessed Virgin and other devout women, when suddenly they heard a great noise as of a mighty wind from heaven, which filled the whole house. This sign of the coming of the Holy Ghost was to awaken their attention. It came suddenly, to convince us that

He visits us out of His pure mercy, and when He pleases. It came from heaven, to show His inspirations are not of this earth. It was vehement, to prove the ardour with which He impels us to all good works; and it filled the whole house, because He presents His gifts to all men and in all places. This wind also represents the breathing of Divine grace upon our souls, to give and preserve their spiritual life. And it is thus the Spouse in the Canticle prays Him to breathe upon the garden of her soul, that the trees of virtue He has planted there may push forth their sweet-scented buds, and be loaded with fruit agreeable to Him."

"And was this wind really the Holy Ghost Himself?" asked Nina.

"Certainly not," answered the pilgrim; "the wind which the Apostles heard, and the tongues of fire which they saw, were but the visible signs of His invisible presence among them."

"A dove, then, was the visible sign of His invisible presence at the baptism of Jesus, was it not?" observed Minette.

"Yes," he replied; "and a dove is beautifully expressive of the innocence which the waters of baptism shed over the soul. But he manifested Himself to the Apostles under the form of fire, as a fitter emblem of Divine love, because it cleanses and transforms into itself all that it subdues."

"And the fire was in the shape of tongues, I suppose," said Minette, "to show them the gift of love was not intended for themselves alone, but was also by their means to be imparted to others."

"True," said the pilgrim; "the clefts in these tongues likewise pointed out the gift of languages, which they received for this purpose. And some of the holy Fathers have remarked on this subject, that as the pride of the men who built the tower of Babel was the source of the division of languages, so the humility of the disciples, who were to found the Christian Church, was the cause of their reunion. 'The spirit of pride out of one tongue made many,' says a great Saint; 'but the Holy Ghost, who is a spirit of simplicity, reunited them for the conversion of the world.'"

"I think the courage with which the Apostles were endowed directly after the descent of the

Holy Ghost quite as wonderful as the miracu
lous gift of tongues," Minette observed. " St.
Peter, who, a little while before, had denied
his Master at the voice of a maid-servant, now
preached Christ Jesus crucified before thousands of the Jews and other nations, assembled at Jerusalem."

" Yes," said the pilgrim; "Christ Himself
had compared the Apostles, for their timidity
and defencelessness, to a flock of sheep in the
midst of wolves; and now these fearful, igno-
rant men confessed Him boldly before kings
and princes; silenced, by their sublime wisdom, the doctors of the Jewish law and the
orators of the Gentiles; and, having in the
space of twelve years converted all the neighbouring nations, they divided the whole world
among them, each taking a share of kingdoms
to himself, that the light of faith might be
carried into every nation on the face of the
earth."

" Please, master pilgrim," asked Nina, " did
our Blessed Lady receive the Holy Ghost as
well as the Apostles?"

" Surely she did, my child, and in a much

greater degree, since the Divine Spirit ever bestows itself most abundantly on the soul most prepared for His visit. And what heart so prepared as the heart of our Blessed Mother? He must be pure who would receive the Holy Ghost; and hers was a purity that had never known a stain—his thoughts must be lifted above the desires of this world; and hers were ever in heaven with her dear Son Jesus—he must be ready to sacrifice all things, and to suffer death itself, for the faith that is within him; and for the establishment of that very faith, she had given her only Son; and had died with Him in spirit at the foot of the Cross,—a death more painful to the heart of the Mother, than ever was fire or sword to the bodies of the martyrs."

"And must we have all these good dispositions when we receive confirmation?" said Madeleine, hesitatingly.

"We must certainly be pure, that is, free from the guilt of mortal sin; and if we do not feel within ourselves the other dispositions, we must desire, at least, and pray earnestly for them. And God, who understands our weak

ness far better than we do ourselves, will, I
doubt not, accept of our good wishes, and will
grant them to us when we are called on to
exert them."

"But we shall never be called on to become
martyrs," said Nina; "for no one is ever put
to death in this country for being Catholics."

"We shall not perhaps have to suffer mar-
trydom in the body," replied the pilgrim "but
we shall have to resist our natural inclinations
to sin, and this is a kind of spiritual martyr-
dom far more difficult to endure. It is in the
hour of temptation we shall prove to ourselves
that we have really received the Holy Ghost;
not indeed, as the Apostles did, with the ex-
ternal gifts of miracles and tongues, but with
the interior graces which give us strength to
resist and overcome the devil, the world, and
ourselves, the most dangerous and unconquer-
able of all our foes."

"And shall we really receive the Holy Ghost,
just as the Apostles did, in confirmation?" asked
Marie.

"Not *visibly*," said the pilgrim, "but *invisi-
bly* He will most certainly descend into our

souls; for Christ has promised that He will abide with the Church forever. He descends upon *all;* but He gives Himself to *each*, just in proportion to the ardour with which He has been sought. The child, therefore, who prepares her soul for this divine guest, by trying to lessen the number of her daily faults, by little practices of mortification, by earnest desire, and fervent prayer, will certainly receive a greater share of His gifts and graces than one who has felt indifferent and careless on the subject."

"I must try and think of all this," said Madeleine; "for, do you know, I am to be confirmed next year. Father Pierre told me so the other day."

"Do so, my dear child," said Minette; "and remember that because you can only receive this sacrament once, it is all the more needful to receive it with the proper dispositions."

"Happy indeed is the young girl," continued the pilgrim, "who invites the Holy Ghost into her heart by innocence of life and fervent desire. He will communicate Himself to her in all His plenitude of heavenly graces; He will bestow upon her the seven gifts of His spirit, by which her understanding will be raised, and her will made strong to the practice of heroic virtue. And from thence will gush forth, as from a fountain, those twelve most precious fruits which show forth His habitual presence within the soul : 'charity,' by which she loves God, and her neighbour for the sake of God ; 'joy,' by which she rejoices in Him ; 'peace,' 'patience,' and 'longanimity,' by which she endures exterior evils with interior calmness nothing can disturb ; 'benevolence,' which is the will to do good ; and 'benignity,' or the execution of that will ; 'mildness,' by which she bears all injuries ; 'fidelity,' by which she hates all deceit and unfaithfulness ; 'modesty' and 'chastity,' by which she regulates her thoughts, and words, and actions ; and lastly, 'continency,' by which she learns to restrain within the strictest bounds of temperance ever the most lawful gratification of her senses."

"I have read somewhere," said Minette, "that many holy persons have imagined the Holy Ghost first appeared over the head of our Blessed Lady, in the visible form of a flame, which afterwards divided itself into tongues of fire, and descended on the Apostles."

"It is a good and holy thought, at any rate," he answered; "since a great preacher has declared, that God wills every good gift should come to us through Mary. When, therefore, these dear little ones are preparing for confirmation, they should often go to this good Mother, and tell her, that as by her means they have received their salvation in Jesus Christ, so they hope by her intercession to obtain the full measure of their santification in the visit of the Holy Ghost, who, if properly received, will make their souls as a 'garden full of delight,' abiding with them in virtue and good works to the end of their days."

"Did our Blessed Saviour receive the Holy Ghost when He appeared at His baptism in the form of a dove?" asked Nina.

"No, my child; Jesus could not receive the Holy Ghost, for He was filled with Him from the beginning. This was but an outward manifestation of His interior presence in the soul of our divine Lord, whereas, in His descent upon the Apostles, He communicated himself to men who did not possess Him before ; and with Himself He gave them full knowledge and understanding of every article of Christian faith necessary for salvation ; as Christ prom ised, when He said, 'He will teach you all things, and bring all things to your mind, whatsoever I shall have said to you.''

Madame Drisbach contrived to make her guests both old and young very happy that evening, and there was much fun and laugh-ter as she cross-examined the school-children concerning their pretensions to be considered as queen of the day, and to wear the wreath of roses which she held in her hand, ready for the coronation.

Nina knew very well she had no chance from the beginning ; for she was such a giddy little thing, that she was always in disgrace either with her school-mistress or her companions. Madeleine would certainly have been chosen, had it not been for a habit of indolence which she had not yet succeeded in completely sub-duing. She acknowledged this very candidly but good-humouredly declared " she would cer-

tainly be queen next Pentecost, as she expect
ed to become a strong and perfect Christian by
the sacrament of confirmation, and then she
would no longer have any difficulty in acqui-
ring habits of activity." She gave her vote for
Marie; and every one instantly agreed that no
one was so worthy of the wreath of roses.
But when Madame Drisbach drew the little
girl towards her, in order to place it on her
head, she caught hold of both her hands, and
said eagerly, "Oh, madame, there is one here
ten times better than I, or any of us; will you
let me bring her?" And, without waiting for
an answer, she darted through the crowd, and
returned with poor little Annette, who had remained at the outside of the circle, little dream-
ing of the honour to which she was to be elected.

Madame Drisbach smiled as she said, "You
are right, Marie."

"Yes, indeed," said Marie; "she has lived
for two years under Master Pippo, whom every
one knows to be a cruel master; and she allowed him to beat her and abuse her as if she had
been a dog, in order to earn food and clothing
for her grandmother and she was up early,

and down late; but Elise told me she never
yet knew her to miss her morning and evening
prayers; and when she came home at night
she was always cheerful and good humored,
and used to make her grandmother's bed, and
to mend her clothes, and get ready her meals
for the next day, just as if she was not quite
weary and over-worked, running after the sheep.
It is very easy for me to be good, because I
am happy, and every one loves me; but Annette has had to be patient in the midst of
troubles, with no one to comfort or say a word
to encourage her."

Madame Drisbach placed her crown on the
head of the astonished shepherdess, and said:

"The virtue which has been proved in difficulty is certainly the most deserving of reward.
And as for you, dear little Marie, you have done
an act of justice which will be the source of greater happiness to you whenever you think of it
than all the roses in the garden could possibly
have been. And now, Annette, what is your
petition? Remember I have promised to grant
it, if it be reasonable.

"If you please, madame," said Annette, stam

mering, " if you would forgive Master Pippo.
He told me this morning you had turned him
out of his employment; and though he was
not very kind to me, still he saved us many a
day of want by the work he gave me."

The Countess shook her head. " No, Annette, that is not a reasonable request; it is generous in you to ask his pardon, but it would not
be just in me to grant it. You must think of
something else."

" Well, then," cried Annette, with a sudden
look of recollection, " you have got a beautiful
bird, madame; I saw it one day at your draw-
ing-room window."

" What! do you want the parrot, Annette?
I fear you would find it an expensive compan
ion," said the smiling Countess.

" No, madame, I don't want the bird, but the
cage. I have two doves for Marie, but have
only a wicker-basket to keep them in, and it
is so dark for the poor little things."

Madame Drisbach spoke a few words to one
of her servants who stood near listening to the
proceedings; and in a few minutes he returned
with a beautiful cage, from which the parrot

had been dislodged by her directions. "And now, Annette, where are the doves?"

"I have them under the foot of yonder tree, madame;" and the shepherdess ran to the spot, and soon came back with an old wicker-basket, from whence she produced two young doves, which rested quite tame and lovingly on her little rough hands.

"O what beautiful creatures!" cried Marie. "Are they really for me, dear Annette?"

"Yes, to be sure, Marie; you gave up your lamb for me; so, when I found these creatures deserted in their nest, I took them home, and nursed them for you."

"But they are even better than the lamb," cried the delighted Marie, "for by this time it has grown almost into a sheep; but these little things will always be just as nice and small as they are now."

"Well," said Madame Drisbach, "I am glad gratitude is one of your good qualities, Annette. And now, since you will ask nothing for yourself, I must tell you that, as a reward for your good conduct, I intend to give the cottage next to Madeleine's to your gaudmother to live in

and, as I think you would not like to leave
your old employment, you shall take care of
the flocks under my new shepherd, who will
pay you double what you received from
Pippo, and will neither beat you nor abuse
you, my poor little girl."

Tears of gratitude were in the child's eyes as
she kissed Madame Drisbach's hand, and then
she took the crown of roses from her head.

" Do wear it, Marie ; it will look nice on
your smooth hair, and mine is as rough and
shaggy as the wool of the old sheep."

" No, indeed," said Marie ; " but perhaps
Madame Drisbach will let us put it on the
image of our Blessed Lady, which I see in
yonder grotto."

Madame Drisbach assented ; and, followed
by her and all the children, Marie brought
the wreath and placed it on the head of a
beautiful Madonna which stood in a kind of
niche cut in the rock, and sheltered by a
graceful drapery of vines. Then, as if moved
by a single impulse, every one knelt down,
and Madame Drisbach said aloud the " Salve
Regina" to this good Mother, who was thus

chosen, by unanimous consent, to be "Lady and Queen of the day."

Their election being thus happily made, the merry party sat down to their supper in the open air; and Madame Drisbach withdrew after seeing that every one was served to his or her satisfaction.

"Here comes the pilgrim," said Nina, as she finished her supper; "but how grave he looks, and he has got his long staff in his hand, which, he says, he never uses except on a journey."

"He is going to tell us his history," cried several voices; and in a few minutes the old man was surrounded by a number of curious faces, all anxious to discover the mystery of his previous acquaintance with Madame Drisbach.

"Sit down, my friends," said he; "and let the children come next to me. I know some among you, though you do not know me; for all have forgotten, it seems, the son of the old Count Drisbach's steward."

"What, young Frank, who left the village when quite a boy? No, indeed, we have not forgotten him. Is it possible you are young Frank?" cried several voices; and many of the older villagers pressed forward to shake the pilgrim by the hand.

" Wait a moment, my friends. You now know *who* I am ; but wait until you know *what* I am, before you offer me your hands in friend· ship. My children," he continued, addressing the wondering little ones aronnd him, "to you in particular I address my story, since it contains a lesson which you cannot learn too soon. The smallest sin deliberately committed may, and too often does, lead us to crimes of the darkest dye. You will perhaps believe this, when I con· fess to you that my first theft was of a copper coin ; my last was of a casket of jewels of ines· timable value. As a child, I was fond of money, and the habit of stealing it in small quantities grew gradually upon me ; and, unhappily for me, it never was discovered. When I was about sixteen, as many here may remember, my father died ; and I left the village, tc ac· company my young master, the late Count, on his travels. While in England, he married the present Countess, then only fifteen years of age ; and instead of returning to Drisbach, tkey took up their residence upon bis German estates. The love of money was still strong upon me; and in order to gratify this evil passion, I took to gambling; but as I was always unfortunate at play, my funds were soon reduced so low, that in order to continue my bad habit, I used to help myself out of my master's purse, to which, as his steward, I had free access. I never did this without some compunctious visitings, and some intention of returning the money when I had regained my losses at play. But that time never came. I lost continually; and at last my companions, who were well acquainted with my petty robberies, threatened to disclose them to the Count, if I did not instantly discharge my debt, which now amounted to a sum much too large to be taken without detection from the money I held for my master. Thus driven to desperation, I suddenly remembered a casket of jewels I had often seen standing on a table in my lady's private sitting-room. In order to make you understand this part of my story, I must tell you that her room opened into the bedchamber of her only child, and this again communicated by a back staircase with the lower part of the house. My lady's whole

soul was wrapt up in her child : it was very
delicate, and subject to fits, from one of which
it was just recovering ; and the physician had
forbidden any one to approach that wing of
the castle, as the least noise or fright might
startle it into a fresh attack ; which, they said,
would certainly prove fatal.   As I have said,"
continued the pilgrim, passing his hand across
his brow, "I thought upon this fatal casket.
It was the evening hour ; my lady was at
vespers, and the nurse who watched the child
most probably asleep.   I stole into the room,
and my hand was on the casket, when some
one tried to open the door by which I had
entered.   My conscience told me I had no
business to be there at such a time ; and, still
holding the casket in my hands, I rushed into
the child's bedroom.   Never shall I forget the
terrible scream which it gave as I entered ; for
months afterwards it rang in my ears ; but at
the moment I only thought of my own preservation ; and dashing through the other door,
I ran to the stables, saddled a horse, and was
soon many a mile on my way to another land.
When I reached England, I turned the ill-got

ten diamonds into gold, traded upon them, made a large fortune, married a wife, and all the world said I was a happy and prosperous man. They knew not what they said. My own conscience was within me; God was above me; and not for an instant could I ever feel happy. At last His avenging hand fell heavily upon me. I doted on my children, but one by one they faded away, and no one could tell me of what malady they died; but I knew it well myself: it was of the just anger of God! My wife was the next victim; my fortune followed; one of those sudden reverses which so frequently happen in trade fell upon me, and from a prince in fortune I became a beggar.

"I will spare you the agony of my late repentance. In the first hour of despair, I believe I should have destroyed myself, had it not been for the kindness of the priest who had attended the deathbeds of my wife and children. He took me to his home. watched over, soothed, and consoled me, until at last he enkindled within me a fervent desire of doing penance for my crimes. It was then I resolved on making a pilgrimage to Jerusalem, to implore the forgiveness of my God on the very spot where He had bought it for me by His blood. Nothing could divert me from my purpose; and with my staff in my hand, and wallet on my shoulder, I begged my way from town to town, from nation to nation, until at length I reached the city rendered holy for ever by the footsteps of a God made man. Many years I spent in that land of the promise and its fulfilment. I traced the life of my crucified Saviour, from Bethlehem, where He was born, to Nazareth, where He dwelt in His childhood; from Gethsemane, where He first drank of the chalice of His Passion, to Mount Calvary, where He drained it even to the dregs. And every day, and every hour of the day, I implored His pardon, by all that He once had said, and done, and suffered for my soul. But still I felt I had not done enough: my crime was greater than my penance for it; therefore I returned to Europe, resolved, in the face of the whole world, to publish my shame, and to ask pardon at the feet of my injured employers. I reached Rome

in the beginning of Holy Week; and there I
learned that my mistress, childless and a widow,
had been living for many years. I could not
bring myself to seek her in her own home;
but I was told she was one of those who attended at the hospital for pilgrims on Maun-
day-Thursday. Thither I went, to await her
coming; and I felt I should know her among
a thousand others. All day long I stood at
the gates; and many went and many came,
but not the one for whom I waited. At last,
towards the dusk of evening, she appeared;
and in her calm eyes and pallid face I read
the history of the childless mother. How she
recognized me I cannot tell; but she did so
instantly; for she drew back, and said faintly,

"'You here?'

"Scarcely knowing what I did, I fell at her feet
and sought her pardon. She advanced a step towards me, and said, in a scarcely audible voice

"'My friend, you have long been forgiven.'

"'One word more,' I cried, gasping for
breath—'the child!' There was a long and
terrible pause, and then she said, in a tone of
unearthly sweetness,

" ' My God! I thank Thee that Thou hast taken it to heaven.'

" I had been certain of its death before, and yet it seemed as if I heard it now for the first time, so awful did it sound from the lips of the mother ; and I wrung my hands in utter despair.   Yet nearer drew that saint of sorrow, and yet more softly did she say,

" ' Be patient, friend ! The little one is happy. It looketh on the face of its heavenly Father !'

" ' Alas! you know not that I am its murderer !'

" ' I know all.   Within the hour of your flight, it died in my arms.'

" ' And yet you pardon !' I could say no more.   I heard her whisper to herself, ' My God! I thank Thee for this hour.'   And then she spoke once more, in a low but earnest voice :

" ' In washing the feet of the worn out pilgrim this day, I have sought to walk in the footsteps of my crucified Jesus.   Shall I refuse to follow Him yet farther, or shall I deny pardon to the penitent heart, when He had no reproaches to offer the treacherous Judas ?'

" Her hands were in mine, as she spoke, to

raise me from the ground, and what happened afterwards I cannot tell ; all I know is, that she took me to her palace, and during the fever which followed, caused by over-excitement of mind and body, she watched and cared for me as if she saw in me, not the destroyer of her child, but a suffering representative of her suffering Saviour. When I recovered, she wished me to come here and take up my abode at the castle. I have come, not indeed for that purpose, but in order to set the seal upon my repentance, by declaring my guilt to the friends of my childhood."

The pilgrim hid his face in his hands as he finished speaking ; and with many an expression of pity and comfort, the astonished villagers drew close around him, when the Countess and Father Pierre returned to the spot. As soon as he saw her, he rose, fell on his knees before her, and said,

"Madame, in obedience to your wishes, I have visited this place ; but I cannot remain. My heart is still in the land where Jesus sorrowed and died for my sins. There would I weep over them during the remainder of my days ; there would I meet death as an atonement for their greatness. I implore you, then once more to say you forgive me, and to let me depart."

"May God forgive me as I forgive you with all my heart and with all my soul," sai. the Countess, earnestly; "and may the sweet Jesus be with you wherever you go!"

"I thank you, dear lady, and you beloved little ones," he said, addressing the children; "may the story you have heard this day be a warning to you. Oh, beware of wilful sin, however venial; you know not how soon it may lead you to that which is mortal. He alone who stills the waves, and makes the storm cease its muttering, can stay the progress of sin once freely admitted into the soul. My children, believe one who knows it from sad experience. The innocence of penance we must purchase for ourselves in shame, in sorrow, and in tears; while that of baptism is a gratuitous gift of God, full of delight, and easy of preservation. Remember that no enjoyment that sin can yield us is worth one hour of the innocence by which it must be purchased."

The pilgrim laid his hand upon Marie's head

as he finished speaking, and drawing his broad-
leafed hat yet deeper over his brows, he walked
rapidly away, and was soon out of sight. The
villagers then expressed their feelings in many
broken exclamations of " Poor fellow ! what a
terrible story ! but he has repented ; he is very
much to be pitied."

" Yes," said Father Pierre, " he has repented ;
he has received a grace which has often been
denied to a thousand others. But you cannot
ponder too long upon his words, or remember
them too well. Venial sin does not indeed de-
stroy the soul, but it ' grieves the Holy Spirit
of God,' and should therefore be avoided as the
worst of evils. And whenever we unhappily fall
into it, we should arise without delay, and go to
our heavenly Father, who knows the weakness
of our human nature, and will readily grant us
forgiveness, for the sake of His dear Son Jesus,
in whose name we implore it. And do you,
dear children, who are indeed innocent by baptism, but not yet made strong by the grace of
confirmation, make it your daily prayer that,
when the Holy Ghost visits you in this sacrament, He may bring with Him all the interior

graces by which He transformed twelve poor fishermen into preachers, apostles, confessors, and martyrs."

"And for us," said Minette, sorrowfully, "who have already received confirmation, and not, perhaps, so worthily as we might have done?"

"Not alone in confirmation," said Father Pierre, "does the Holy Ghost descend upon men. Every day and every hour He will visit us, if we will only take care to invite Him. Keep your heart pure, and He will make it His temple. Implore His divine presence in your soul, and He will 'fill it with brightness; He will make it like a watered garden, and like a fountain of water, whose waters shall not fail. Then shall you go on your way rejoicing; and when death approaches, you shall not be afraid, but shall be glad that the hour is arrived for your eternal union with that Spirit of love which Jesus Christ purchased for us by His death, and which first descended upon mankind in the persons of the Apostles, replenishing them with all grace and sweetness and power and wisdom on the high and holy festival of Pentecost."

JESU, I MY CROSS HAVE TAKEN.

JESU,—I my cross have taken,
　　All to leave and follow Thee;
I am poor, despised, forsaken,—
　　Thou henceforth my all shalt be:
Perish every fond ambition,—
　　All I've sought, or hoped, or known;
Yet how rich is my condition,—
　　God and heaven may be mine own!

Let the world despise and leave me,
　　It has left my Saviour too;
Human hearts and looks deceive me,
　　Thou art not like them untrue:
Whilst thy graces shall adorn me,
　　God of wisdom, love, and might,—
Foes may hate, and friends may scorn me;
　　Show thy face, and all is bright.

Go then,—earthly fame and treasure,
　　Come, disaster, scorn, and pain;
In thy service, pain is pleasure,—
　　With thy favor, loss is gain.
I have called Thee, Abba Father!
　　I have set my heart on Thee:
Storms may howl, and clouds may gather,
　　All will work for good to me.

Man may trouble and distress me,
 'Twill but drive me to thy breast;
Life with trials hard may press me,
 Heaven will bring me sweeter rest
Oh, 'tis not in grief to harm me,
 While thy love is left to me;—
Oh, 'twere not in joy to charm me
 Were that joy unmixed with Thee!

Soul,—then know thy full salvation,
 Rise o'er sin, and fear, and care;
Joy to find in every station,
 Something still to do or bear.
Think what spirit dwells within thee,
 Think what sacraments are thine;
Think that Jesus died to win thee:
 Child of heaven, canst thou repine?

Haste thee on from grace to glory,
 Arm'd with faith and wing'd with prayer
An eternal day before thee
 Waits for God to guide thee there.
Soon shall close thine earthly mission,
 Patience shall the spirit raise;
Hope shall change to glad fruition,
 Faith to sight, and prayer to praise!